To Alberic and Rose

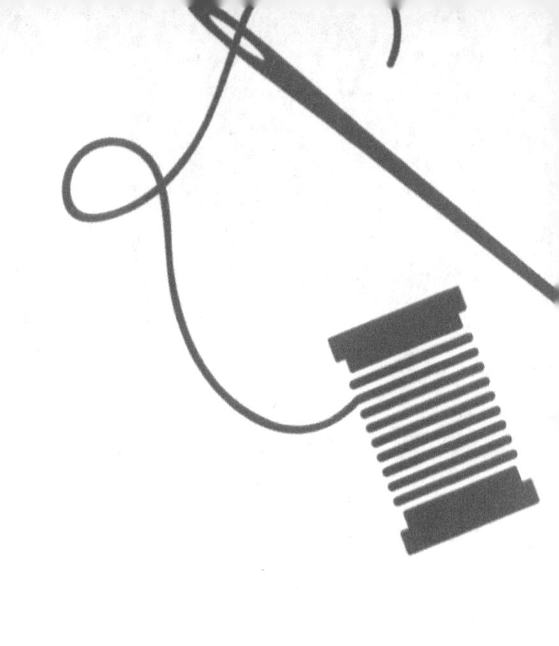

Table of Contents

Prologue

María stared at her reflection in the mirror. Her hair was coiffed perfectly for the veil's positioning on her head. Abuela had asked Señora Medina to make the dress. Every detail on the dress was so unique, so intricate. The embroidery on the veil made her eyes water. She had never worn anything so beautiful. María wiped the tears from her eyes, forgetting she was wearing white gloves.

"María! Don't dirty the gloves before the ceremony!" Abuela exclaimed as she grabbed María's hands to inspect them. "Everything must be perfect. White as snow. Pure." She cupped María's cheeks with her hands. "You look beautiful, mi Angelita." María looked at her grandmother with affection. She lived to please her, and today she finally saw approval in her grandmother's eyes.

Suddenly the bathroom door opened, and a thin middle-aged nun said, "Everyone is ready, María. It is time."

A dozen butterflies were set free in María's stomach at the sound of Sister Lupe's announcement. It was time. For María, it was the day she had always dreamed of.

It was the day that she would stand before family and friends and profess her love.

"Hurry now, María. I have to run to my seat. I'll see you after the ceremony."

María watched her grandmother scurry out of the bathroom toward the sanctuary. She then took a deep breath and set out after her to take her place in the processional. Her best friend, Ana, was already positioned in front of her.

"I can't wait until after the ceremony for the reception," Ana said. "It's going to be so much fun!"

Ana always had a way of being the center of attention. Even on a day like today, she found a way to make it all about her. Nonetheless, María loved her. She was happy Ana could be a part of this day.

The music started playing on the grand organ, "Ave María," the perfect song choice. As María walked down the aisle, her heart beat so fast and hard that she found it hard to keep the cadence. Although it seemed that all eyes were on her, María kept her eyes locked on the altar. The only people that mattered at this moment were standing up there.

As the music came to a halt and María took her place at the front of the church, she looked back and saw Abuela sitting in the front pew. Her grandmother's smile warmed her heart. It wasn't often that she could get that woman to exercise the muscles in her face.

Father Lopez startled her as his baritone voice projected throughout the church, "In the name of the Father, and of the Son, and of the Holy Spirit." María quickly looked forward in anticipation for his next words.

"We have come together today to celebrate the sacrament of Holy Communion."

María smiled and whispered to herself, "Yes . . . To celebrate my marriage to Jesus!"

Chapter 1

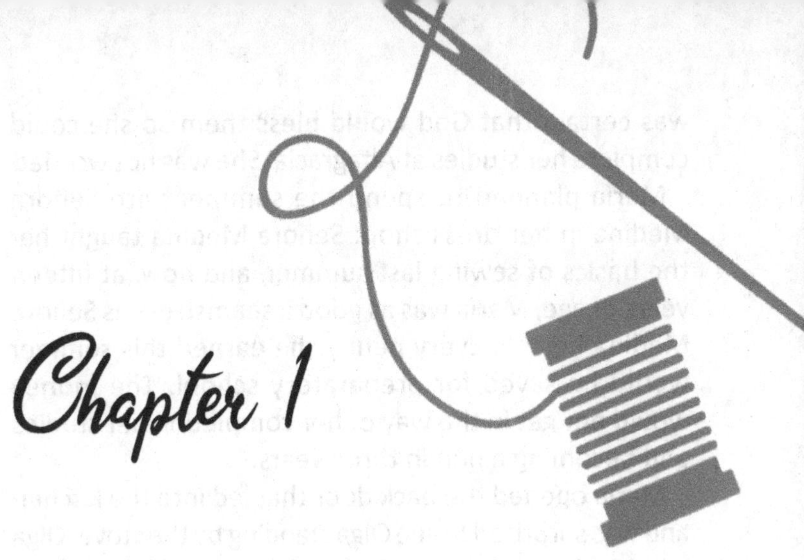

SEVEN YEARS LATER . . .

María sat outside while everyone was still asleep. It was her routine to wake up before the rooster crowed to say her Rosary prayers. This was the only time she had to spend alone in prayer. Although her family loved the Lord and attended Mass weekly, María was the only one who radically expressed her faith and attended Mass daily.

A bang inside the house let María know that her quiet time was over. Soon Abuela would be shouting orders for everyone to get started on chores. Things would be different in three months. María was accepted into Nuestra Señora de la Altagracia Convent Preparatory School to complete secondary education. Abuela could not afford to send her there for the first year, but after many appeals and María working the last year cleaning the convent once a week, she was accepted in with a one-year scholarship. "We'll worry about payment for your third year when it comes," Abuela would say. María was certain that God would bless them so she could complete her studies at Altagracia. She was not worried.

María planned to spend the summer with Señora Medina in her dress shop. Señora Medina taught her the basics of sewing last summer, and now, at fifteen years of age, María was as good a seamstress as Señora Medina herself. Every penny she earned this summer would be saved for preparatory school. The money would not get in the way of her completing her studies and becoming a nun in three years.

María opened the back door that led into the kitchen and was surprised to see Olga standing by the stove. Olga was María's older sister. She had dreams of becoming a nurse, but the cost of nursing school in the city was too expensive. After she graduated from secondary school, she stayed at home to help Abuela run the house and wait for a suitor. It's been over four years, and not one man has come to the house inquiring about Olga. María knew that Olga resented her, though Olga never verbally expressed it. All the effort was made for her to go to the convent, but nothing was done to make a way for Olga to attend nursing school. If Olga had moved to the city for school, surely, within a month, someone would have been at Abuela's door asking for Olga's hand in marriage. Instead, she remained in the small town with no prospects and little hope for a happy life. After all, she was twenty-two years old. In a couple of years, she would be considered an old hag.

"I don't understand why you are the first one up every morning, yet I am the one who has to prepare breakfast for everyone!" Olga barked when María came in.

"You choose to make the breakfast, Olga. No one said you had to," María replied sarcastically. Although Olga was older than her, María never allowed her to speak to her harshly without putting up a fight.

"Have you ever considered being patient and letting someone else get a chance to make the meal instead of jumping right in and complaining about it?" María asked as she rolled her eyes.

"Fine!" Olga shouted as she slammed the pan on the stove. She raised her hands in a sign of surrender and said, "You make breakfast. It's all yours." As she walked away, she looked over her shoulder and, with a smirk, said, "Oh, and don't forget to get the eggs from the chickens outside in the coop, Hermanita."

María's face felt hot, and she had to remind herself to stay calm and be "nun-like." Olga always knew what button to press to get her worked up. María knew she couldn't give Olga the power to control her emotions. She would just get the eggs out of that dreaded coop and make the best breakfast the family ever had.

As María prepared the rest of the menu, someone knocked on the back door. It was Señora Medina. Abuela came out of her room, annoyed that someone would come calling at this time in the morning.

"Please forgive me for stopping by so early," Señora Medina pleaded.

"What's wrong, Estela?" Abuela said, suddenly concerned. "I have never seen you so anxious before."

"I have an emergency in the city," Señora Medina began. "I must go there for the day to handle some business. Normally, I would shut down the shop to the public and keep my seamstresses working in the back, but I have an important appointment today with the Morales family. I cannot cancel."

Abuela looked dumbfounded at Señora Medina, still trying to figure out what this had to do with them.

"María," Señora Medina continued with little air in her lungs, "I need you to work in the front today and handle the appointment for me."

María's face turned pale. "Señora Medina, there are many other older ladies who can handle the front area," María pleaded. "I am only fifteen. I think it would be better if you asked someone else."

"I agree," Abuela retorted. "You can't give such a responsibility to a child. It is not wise, Estela."

"With all due respect, María is quite capable of handling this task. She is far better than any of my other seamstresses combined, and she can take the order just as well as if I were there. I trust her." Señora Medina paused, knowing she wasn't convincing them yet. "And I will pay her double for the day."

María's eyes lit up. More money for her school fund; she couldn't possibly refuse that. Clearly, this was a gift from the heavens. She turned to Abuela and tried to read the stone look on her face. "Well, Abuela?" María whispered.

"Well, what? Yes! Of course! How can you say no? Señora Medina needs you!"

Señora Medina and María burst into laughter at Abuela's sudden change of heart.

"Bueno!" Señora Medina said in between chuckles. "Be there by 10:00 am to help get the team started. The appointment is at noon. I'll be back by 3:00."

"Gracias, Señora. Thank you for this opportunity. I won't let you down," María said confidently.

"I know you won't," Señora Medina replied as she walked out the back door. "That's why I chose you."

María and Abuela stood by the door and watched Señora Medina until she drove away in her car. Suddenly, when the car was barely visible, the two of them burst into laughter again. María laughed so hard tears rolled down her cheeks. Olga ran into the kitchen yelling, "What's all the noise about in here?" putting a damper on the mood.

"Olga, where have you been?" Abuela exclaimed. "Get breakfast started already!"

Before Olga could utter a word, María added, "Yeah, Olga, I think the chickens also have some eggs ready for you out there." María patted Olga on the back as she walked away and whispered, "I like mine scrambled, Hermanita."

Sol y Luna was a small store in town that Señora Medina purchased several years ago. She used to make clothes out of her house but was forced to purchase space and hire help when her business took off after the war. The majority of the building was used as a factory where fifteen seamstresses came in and made garments based on client orders. On the rare occasions when business was slow, Señora Medina would design something new and make several of each size to sell to the major department stores in the city.

In the front of the store were displayed sample garments, along with a variety of fabrics. Señora Medina did not want to stop that portion of her business when she expanded. She still wanted people to come in and order specialty-made clothing made just for them. To have an outfit made by Señora Medina was becoming a big thing, and her price changes reflected as such.

Señora Medina worked day and night over the years to become what she was today. Although she wasn't married or had any children, she was content with her life and independence. She would always say, "Men are only road blocks to your dreams and goals. I can do without them". Nonetheless, for business purposes, she wanted to be referred to as Señora Medina, as if she were married. She gained more respect that way.

María worked in the back with the team, thirteen ladies and one gentleman, Ramón Castillo. Ramón took pride in his work but was not very personable with the clients. His customer service was horrible. In his mind, the customer was never right. Ramón's flamboyant and artistic demeanor fanned the town gossiper's flames daily. Although he was widowed with grown children in college in the city, the rumors were that he lived an alternative lifestyle. María loved Ramón. He didn't care what people said about him and never felt the need to defend himself. "God knows who I am, and so does my Claudia—may she rest in peace. That's all that matters."

Time flew by working with Ramón. Before she knew it, María heard the bell signaling that the front door opened. It was noon, the Morales appointment. María stood up and quickly whispered a Hail Mary as she adjusted her dress. She wanted to make sure she got one more prayer in before this important task. She couldn't mess this up. Señora Medina was counting on her.

When María confidently walked through the curtains that separated the front room from the work stations, she was greeted by a tall woman and a toddler. "Hola! Welcome to Sol y Luna. May I help you?"

"Sí, my name is Ines Morales. I have an appointment with Señora Medina," the woman said as her eyes searched the room.

"I'm sorry," María started, "Señora Medina had an emergency in the city, but she asked me to take special care of you. My name is María." With a smile on her face,

María extended her hand, but the client simply looked at it and walked away.

"My appointment was with Señora Medina, not with some girl," Señora Morales said calmly yet sharp enough to jab the wrong nerve in María.

"With all due respect, Señora, I am not 'some girl.' I am the seamstress that the owner of this business trusted to handle your request. Again, how may I help you?" Score for María. The client had found her match.

After what seemed like a lifetime of silence, Señora Morales moved to the counter and laid her purse down. María noticed that it was one of those expensive leather purses, nothing like the handmade ones they sold at the market.

"I need to have some outfits made for my son: five trousers, ten shirts, and two blazers," Señora Morales ordered.

"I can help you with that," María said cheerfully. "Let me show you some of our popular children's designs you can choose from."

"Children's?" the woman shouted. "Why would I need to look at those? My son is eighteen years old. He's going to college!"

María looked confused. "I'm sorry. I only assumed you meant for this little boy . . ."

Señora Morales waved her hand and interrupted María. "This is my nephew! My son is across the street at the farmer's market with my sister. You will do better, my dear, not to make assumptions." Score for Señora Morales.

María was already tired of this game. "In that case, Señora Morales, I will wait for your son to come in so he can choose what fabrics and styles he likes." María spoke in a tone that suggested she was unaffected by the woman.

"Did I stutter when I said that I needed to order some outfits?" Señora Morales took a step closer to María. "My opinion is the only one needed here. I am paying for this, not my son." She continued on speaking as she walked around the store. "My son is going to college. I cannot have him looking common—like everyone else. He is a Morales. He is destined for greatness, and that is how he will dress."

María couldn't help but roll her eyes at the client. Thankfully, Señora Morales had turned the other way and didn't see it. Just as María couldn't stomach any more from this woman, the bell rang as the front door opened. In walked a woman who bore a remarkable resemblance to Señora Morales.

"Welcome to Sol y Luna," María recited.

"Hola, niña" the woman replied. "What a beautiful dress you have on!"

María smiled and thanked the woman. Clearly this lady's name should have been Glenda, for she was the good sister. The other one had to be . . .

The bell rang again. This time it was the son . . . the very handsome son. Suddenly, María felt her face warm up. She had never seen such a handsome boy. Her heart did summersaults.

"Hurry up, Antonio," Señora Morales shouted. "I need to see this shade of blue against your skin." María watched as the woman held up the piece of fabric against the Adonis's cheek. She was so focused on him that she didn't notice "Glenda" looking at her.

"Niña," the sister said. "We will need measurements taken. Do you have someone who can do that?" She looked at María and winked.

"Oh, I can do that. I am qualified," María said, stumbling over her words.

"Little girl," the wicked sister retorted. "My son will not have his measurements taken by a teenage girl. It is inappropriate where we come from. Where do you come from?"

María's eyes shifted to Antonio. She could feel her face getting warm again, but this time from embarrassment. María had no quick comeback; Señora Morales scored a three-pointer.

Sensing María's humiliation, the sister walked over to María and spoke softly while caressing her back. "Sweetheart, can you get a man to take my nephew's measurements?"

"Of course," María whispered. "Excuse me for one moment." María ran through the curtains that divided the store and found Ramón standing by the curtains with anger in his eyes.

"I heard everything, niña," Ramón said, hugging her. "You did a great job handling her." As Ramón pulled away, he asked, "Would you like me to take the measurements? Today you are the boss. Tell me what you want."

María's eyes widened, and a wave of confidence came over her. Ramón always made her feel empowered.

Ramón continued, "I could take the measurements and send them on their way, or we can simply just send them on their way. Your choice."

María let out a chuckle and gave Ramón a kiss on the cheek. "Let's take the measurements, Ramón. She doesn't scare me!"

By the time María and Ramón returned to the sales floor, the fabric and styles had been chosen for all garments. Ramón took Antonio's measurements while María wrote up the order. Every time she looked up from the order form, she caught Antonio looking at her. *Does he not speak?* She thought to herself. She made a mental note to add him to her night prayers. With a mother like that, it's no wonder he had no words!

The remainder of the appointment was handled calmly and professionally. Ramón stayed in the front store to keep watch over María.

"Señora Medina will be in touch to discuss pricing," María said and handed Señora Morales a carbon copy of the order.

"Here is a deposit for the order," Señora Morales said as she opened her purse.

"There is no need for that," María said holding her hand up.

"I want to make sure my son's outfits are made with excellence. I'm leaving a deposit." Señora Morales handed María 4000 pesos. María had never held so much money before. She tried not to seem awed by the cash in her hands, but Ramón could tell María was just setting herself up for another round of shots from Señora Morales. Ramón walked up to María and grabbed the money. "I'll put this in the safe for you, Señorita."

María smiled at Ramón. What would she do without him?

Soon after, the appointment was over and the Morales family left. As Antonio walked out the door, he turned around and locked eyes with María one last time. There was that feeling again. She quickly looked away for fear he would see her blush. When María looked up, she saw Ramón watching her. "What's wrong?" María asked like someone who was caught with her hand in the cookie jar.

"Song of Solomon, chapter eight verse four," Ramón replied in a low voice.

"What do you mean?" María replied defensively.

"Tonight, when you go home, look up that scripture and pray." Then Ramón went back through the curtains to his workstation, leaving María bewildered.

A few minutes after, Señora Medina came bursting through the door. "I'm back! How did everything go?"

"María laughed and said, "Aye, Señora! Have I got a story for you!"

Chapter 2

S eñora Medina was more than pleased with the outcome of the Morales appointment. She honored the agreement and paid María double as well all as gave Ramón a bonus after some convincing from María. Señora Medina was able to negotiate a deal with Señora Morales that guaranteed future orders.

After María explained how Señora Morales treated her that day, Señora Media cunningly added 20 percent to the price of the order but offered her a 10 percent coupon off her next order. "Let her pay for her ignorance," Señora Medina sneered.

Three weeks had gone by, and María was able to work extra hours to help with the Morales order. This was the busiest she had ever seen Sol y Luna. Señora Medina's meeting in the city proved to be very profitable for her. The company that normally supplied school uniforms to San Pablo Primary School sustained major flood damage because of a recent storm. They were not able to fulfill a complete order in time for the new school year. Sol y Luna was the vendor of choice to produce one hundred school uniforms for boys and girls. Although it wasn't

Señora Medina's usual line of clothing, she decided to take the opportunity to expand the business and make special departments. Sol y Luna now had a uniform department to manage the repeat business every year. There was also officially a formalwear, menswear, and ladies' casual department.

Ramón was promoted to manage the menswear department. Eventually, with the addition of four new seamstresses, Señora Medina would have to add to the building for more space. María was a little sad to be leaving in September and missing out on all the coming changes to Sol y Luna.

María stopped by the store on her way to church that afternoon to pick up her week's wages. She wanted to have some money to get candles so she could say prayers for Abuela, Olga, and her younger sister, Magdalena. Now and then, María put money in the offering to buy candles to light them up in front of the statue of Mother Mary. María believed her petitions were put on the priority list when she lit candles for Mother Mary. Abuela had pain in her hip for three days. Olga continued to yearn for a husband. Magdalena needed to be more grounded. She was so carefree; she was bound to get in trouble one day and disgrace la familia.

When María walked in the door of Sol y Luna, Ramón was in the front shop with Señora Medina. "What are you doing here, María?" Ramón asked crudely.

Señora Medina gave him a look. "Why so mean, Ramón?"

"I came to pick up my pay, Ramón," María explained, feeling hurt at Ramón's greeting.

He sensed that he came off too strong and tried to soften it up. "I'm sorry, niña. I just thought you were going to the afternoon prayers today at the church. I didn't expect to see you."

María smiled, not sure if she believed his excuse, but nevertheless, he made an effort. "I want to light candles in church. I didn't want to ask Abuela for money."

"No hay problema, María," Señora Medina chimed in. "Your money is right here in this envelope."

Suddenly the fitting room door opened, and out came Antonio Morales. Apparently, he had an appointment for a fitting for his trousers and blazers. María dropped the envelope, surprised to see him again. It seemed she was just able to get him out of her thoughts, and now here he was again.

"María!" Ramón startled her with his loud voice. "You don't want to be late for prayers, do you?"

Baffled by his behavior, María responded. "Of course not. I'm leaving now." María put the envelope in her purse and thanked Señora Medina. She walked out of the store without saying goodbye to Ramón. She didn't understand why he was being so rude to her, and to embarrass her in front of Antonio, nonetheless. María was walking so fast that before she knew it, she was at San Lucas Church. "Get it together, María. This time is for Jesus."

María entered the church and sat in the front row. Sister Ana was leading prayer today. For forty-five minutes, they did the Rosary and sang hymns. When it was all over, María got up to go to the back of the church for the candles. Halfway down the aisle, she noticed a familiar face sitting in the last pew. As she got closer and the face got clearer, her heart beat faster. *He followed me to the church?* It was Antonio Morales. María lowered her head when she realized who it was and continued walking toward the candles.

"I want to apologize," Antonio blurted out when María walked by. María turned to him and pointed to the confessionals. "You can do penance over there."

"No," Antonio exclaimed and grabbed María's arm. "I want to apologize to you for the way my mother treated you a few weeks ago at Sol y Luna. I'm sorry."

María was lost in his voice. For eighteen years of age, he had a deep smooth voice that held sincerity.

Suddenly realizing that she was at church gazing into a boy's eyes, María changed her demeanor. "That's ok. She didn't bother me. I'm the one who's sorry . . . for you!" María turned around, determined to make it to the candles.

"Wait," Antonio replied. "What do you mean?"

Just then, Sister Ana walked by and hushed Antonio for talking loudly. This time it was Antonio's turn to be red in the face, and the look on his face made María giggle. After a moment, they both started to giggle to the point where Antonio grabbed María's hand and ran out of the church. As soon as they ran through the exit doors, the two of them burst out in laughter. When María realized she was still holding Antonio's hand, she broke free and said, "I have to go."

"Stay with me. Let's talk," Antonio said softly. He sat on the steps of the church and motioned to the spot next to him. María was hesitant but figured a quick conversation wouldn't hurt, so she sat down beside him.

"What did you mean when you said you were sorry for me?" Antonio asked again.

"I don't mean to be rude, but your mom . . . I'm sorry you're related to her."

"She's a nice person once you get to know her," Antonio explained. "She's just a perfectionist, that's all."

"Well, I don't intend to be around her long enough to see her nice side," María said, and they both started laughing again.

"I'm going to college in September. Mami just wants me to represent the family well. I am the only child, and they have high expectations for me," Antonio explained. It was almost as if he needed to vent like he had no one in his life to talk to freely.

Antonio went on to talk about his family and how hard his parents worked to live a good life. His mother cleaned houses four days a week for ten hours a day in an upscale town. His father was a plantation manager. He worked twelve hours a day, five days a week, over-seeing dozens of crop pickers at Del Rico Farms. They both made good wages but at the expense of having a true relationship with Antonio.

Many times growing up, Antonio was left with his aunt, Carmelina, because his parents picked up extra shifts at work. Tia Carmelina was very nurturing and attentive with Antonio. She loved him as if he were her own child and always encouraged him to love himself.

"If it wasn't for my aunt, I don't know where I would be," Antonio said. "I tried to run away from home twice before, but she set me straight and sent me back home. 'Pray,' she would say. Pray and let God do His work.'"

"That's good advice," María said softly. "Your aunt is a very nice woman."

Antonio looked at María to respond, but the words wouldn't come out. He could tell that María started to feel uncomfortable by the way he stared. Her cheeks gave it away. "I'm sorry to stare," Antonio said. "You are very beautiful."

María covered her cheeks with her hands. She had never heard that from a boy before, and the way she felt hearing it scared her.

"I . . . I . . . uh . . ." María started to speak but stuttered. "I'm going to be a—" María stopped short when she heard her name being shouted from across the street.

"María!" It was Ramón. Guilt suddenly enveloped her as if she were caught doing something wrong. Ramón was on his bicycle and rode it across the street up to the church.

"María, what are you doing here?" Ramón asked in an accusatory tone.

"Ramón, you know that I came to church for prayers," María answered quickly.

"Yes, but that was hours ago. It is nearly sunset, María." Ramón looked at Antonio, trying to figure out his intentions. "Go home, María. We will talk about this tomorrow."

María felt an anger stir within her. Granted, she had no idea all that time had gone by. Talking to Antonio was so easy and natural. It was as if time stood still. But who was Ramón to tell her what to do?

María went down the steps of the church to talk to Ramón privately. "Ramón, why are you speaking to me this way?" she whispered. "You are not my father. Besides, I am not doing anything wrong."

Ramón stood straight and narrowed his eyes on María. "I may not be your father," he shouted, "but I care for you and your future. You are going to be a nun, María!"

All the color left María's face in that instant. She couldn't bear to turn around to see if Antonio heard what Ramón had said. She stood there motionless, looking at Ramón, fighting back the tears. María could hear Antonio's footsteps going down the steps behind her, and she braced herself for what he would say to her. Suddenly, from the corner of her eye, she noticed him walking down the street. She couldn't believe it. He had just walked away. A tear fell from her eye.

"María," Ramón said softly. "Go home, niña."

María shook her head in obedience and headed home. She took a different route to avoid bumping into Antonio. A flood of emotions came over her, and she couldn't explain why. Besides embarrassment and hurt, she had this overwhelming feeling of guilt. *What did I do wrong? We were only talking.*

Suddenly, as if someone were walking next to her whispering softly, she heard **Song of Solomon. Chapter eight, verse four**. María stopped immediately, searching around for the owner of the voice. It was the same scripture Ramón told her look up, which she never did. Was it her conscious reminding her now?

María ran the rest of the way home, eager to read what was in the verse. As she came up to the house, she saw her younger sister outside playing with a stray cat.

"María!" Magdalena exclaimed. "Abuela's been looking for you."

"Not now, Lena. I have to do my Bible studies," María replied out of breath, running into the house. Magdalena watched her sister, afraid of what would happen next. She tried to warn her that Abuela was angry, but María wouldn't listen.

María went into the house through the back door in an effort to go straight to her bedroom. She took two careful steps, then heard voices in the sitting room. Abuela had guests . . . even better! She could go to her room without being noticed and stay there until bedtime.

"Why don't you come greet our guest?" Abuela said as if she had eyes in the back of her head.

María stood by her bedroom door, afraid to turn around. *How did she know I was here?*

"María," Abuela said again, this time with a more stern tone.

María put a smile on her face and practically skipped to the sitting room in an attempt to make light of the situation.

"Buenas noches," María said as she entered the room and embraced Abuela. She didn't recognize the woman sitting there but gave her a respectful nod hello regardless.

"This is Señora Reyes, María. She works at the bakery across from San Lucas."

María felt her heart in her throat. She knew what would come next.

"María, Señora Reyes thinks she saw you at the church today. Were you there?" Abuela asked.

"Yes, Abuela," María answered.

"But she said she saw you sitting outside on the steps. Were you sitting on the steps, María?"

"Yes, Abuela."

"Here is the part I find hard to believe," Abuela continued. "Señora Reyes said she saw you at church, on the steps outside, talking to a boy! I told her there was no way it was you. Was I right, María?"

"No, Abuela," María answered slowly with her head down.

Señora Reyes stood up at that moment and said, "I must be going now."

Abuela walked her to the door and thanked her for coming. For what? For being the neighborhood watch? María knew better than to move from her spot. She waited for Abuela to come back for her tongue lashing. Abuela did not spank, but she could hurt someone to the core with her words. María braced herself.

"Well, are you going to explain yourself?" Abuela shouted as soon as she closed the front door.

"I wasn't doing anything wrong, Abuela," María cried out. "After Mass, I saw one of Señora Media's customers, and we got into a conversation, and I lost track of time!"

"That must have been a real good conversation since you were late over two hours, María!" Abuela stood with her hands on her hips to emphasize her anger. "What could you have to talk to a boy about for over two hours?"

"Nothing. Everything. We just talked," María said as a single tear fell from her eyes. That feeling of guilt returned, and she didn't know why.

"You are going to be a nun, María," Abuela shouted. "Do you have any idea how bad it looks for people to see you on the steps in a deep conversation with a boy? And on the church steps nonetheless!"

Abuela went on for what seemed to be the longest lecture in the history of lectures. All the while, María kept shaking her head. She couldn't understand what harm was done. When Abuela couldn't talk anymore, she sent María to her room without dinner. "You need to sacrifice your meal and go pray for God's mercy!"

María ran to her room and found Magdalena and Olga in there. They heard everything. The three sisters shared a room, so there was no escaping them and the comments that were surely coming. Magdalena approached María with fear in her eyes. "Are you mad at me?" she asked. María looked at her confused.

"Why would I be mad at you?" María said annoyed.

"I tried to warn you about the lady, but you wouldn't listen to me," Magdalena said worriedly.

"It's not your fault, Lena. You didn't cause the gossiper to come and upset Abuela for no reason," María said as she plopped on her bed.

"Don't be mad at Señora Reyes," Olga chimed in. "She wouldn't have had anything to say if it weren't for you."

"Thank you, Olga," María said. "I can always count on you to bring the last sting." María grabbed her book of novenas on the night stand and began to read.

Song of Solomon. Chapter eight verse four. There it was again, that voice! María decided to put an end to the mystery and look up the Bible verse. She tiptoed into the sitting room to get the family Bible. Most of her books had select scripture in them or were just full of novenas. She needed the complete Bible to look up the scripture. She ran back in the room and quickly searched for Song of Solomon.

> ***I charge you, O daughters of Jerusalem,***
> ***that ye stir not up nor awaken my love***
> ***until he please.***

María read the verse three times, trying to figure would why Ramón would tell her to look it up. "What are you trying to say?" she whispered to herself. As if her question was being answered, the voice inside her said, "You're not ready. Don't look for love there. Seek me first." María quickly sat up in her bed.

"What," Olga exclaimed.

"Didn't you hear that?" María asked anxiously.

"That's just thunder, loca," Olga replied.

She wasn't talking about the thunder. She was talking about the voice. It was so clear and audible this time.

María felt like she was going crazy. She closed the Bible and put it away with her novena books and got ready for bed. She wanted to put this day behind her and start fresh tomorrow. Rest was what she needed. Tomorrow would be a new day, and all would be forgotten.

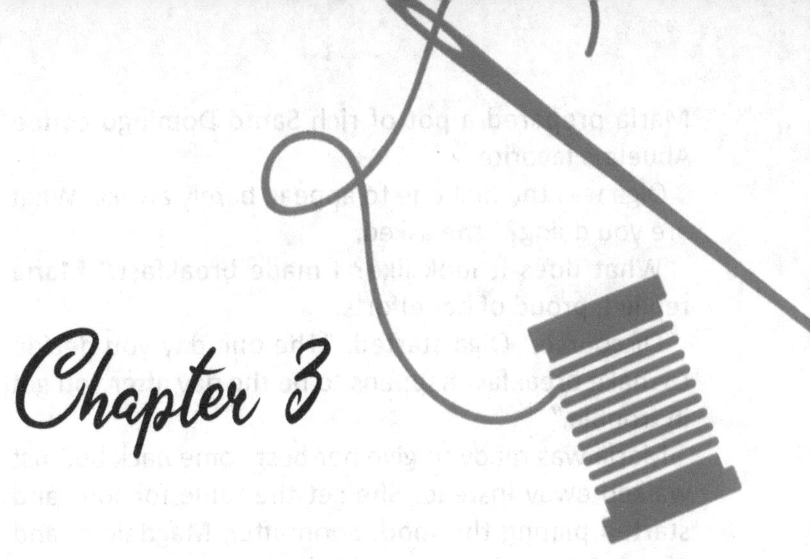

Chapter 3

S unrise came, the rooster crowed, and María just lay in bed. She didn't feel like doing her normal morning prayers. María usually enjoyed the quiet time she spent with God in the early morning, but this day, she simply didn't have the desire.

María lay staring at the ceiling thinking about the scene at the church. How could Ramón blurt out that she was going to be a nun? María wanted to be the one to tell Antonio. She didn't want to admit that she was hurt by the way he just walked away and didn't say a word to her. But what else could he do? The truth was that she would become a nun and would probably never see him again. After all, it was just a conversation, and he was just an acquaintance.

María finally decided to get up and make breakfast for the family. No eggs today, she thought. She wasn't going into that chicken coup ever again. María started a hearty ethnic breakfast that she knew would gain points with Abuela. Mangú, sautéed onions, and fried salami was on the menu. Within thirty minutes, the aroma filled the house, awakening the senses. For a final touch,

María prepared a pot of rich Santo Domingo coffee, Abuela›s favorite.

Olga was the first one to appear, barely awake. What are you doing?" she asked.

"What does it look like? I made breakfast," María replied, proud of her efforts.

"Of course," Olga started. "The one day you decide to make breakfast happens to be the day after you get in trouble."

María was ready to give her best come back but just walked away instead. She set the table for four and started plating the food. Soon after, Magdalena and Abuela joined them in the kitchen.

"Buenos días, Abuela . . . Hermana," María said cheerfully.

"Buenos días, María," Magdalena responded with even more enthusiasm. Her youthful innocence warmed María's heart, though they were not that far in age.

Abuela went straight for the coffee and filled a mug, then poured it down the sink. It was her morning ritual to "give honor to the ancestors," as she would say it. After pouring a second cup, she looked at María. "Everything looks good, María. Muy bien." Approval. María's face lit up, reflecting her joy inside that Abuela was pleased.

Shortly after, the typical chatter began around the table about various topics as they enjoyed the breakfast. "After Mass today, we will go to the farmer's market. They are having a Sunday art festival," Abuela announced.

Magdalena smiled wide and practically leaped out of her chair. "I love the art fest! One day I will showcase my crafts at the festival too."

Magdalena was the artistic one of the three. She dreamed of traveling the world and painting and sculpting everything in sight. They were big dreams for a little country girl from a small island.

María was happy that Abuela was in the mood to go out. Hopefully, that was a sign that she had forgotten all about what happened the day before. They could move forward and put it all behind them and enjoy a Sunday at the festival.

After Mass, the Garcia ladies headed down Cocquina Street toward the farmer's market. Even though there was word that there was a chance of rain, the weather couldn't have been more beautiful. Magdalena was quickly drawn to a section with young artists displaying their talents. She immediately started a conversation with one of the artists about their work. Olga and Abuela wandered down the next aisle of art displays, leaving María alone staring at a sculpture of a woman and her child. Once in a while, María would let her mind escape and wonder what it would be like to be married and have a family. Although she was sure that her future was at the convent, she couldn't help but wonder what it would be to have a child call her "Mami."

The closest thing María knew for a mother was Abuela. When María was very young, her mother died. Abuela never got over losing her daughter, and María and her sisters were forbidden to bring her up in Abuela's presence. That was not a problem for María because she couldn't remember anything about her mother. All she knew was that from the time she was four years old, Abuela had been the one to take care of her and her sisters and be that mother she needed.

The sound of familiar laughter interrupted María's daydreaming. When María searched the crowd, she saw Señora Morales and her sister at the crafts booth. María felt a lump in her throat as she looked for a way to escape. There was something about that woman that made her feel inadequate, and she didn't like that feeling.

Suddenly she felt the arms of a little boy around her legs. Señora Morales' nephew recognized her and ran over to embrace her. *Great . . . no hiding now.*

As if time stopped, and there was a spotlight on her, Señora Morales and her sister slowly approached María. At the same time from another direction, Abuela, Olga, and Magdalena were making their way toward her as well, forcing María to make introductions.

"Buenos días, Señora Morales," María said with barely a smile. "This is my abuela and my two sisters, Olga and Magdalena."

"Ah sí, I've heard about you," Abuela responded quickly. "Buenos días,"

Señora Morales held Abuela's gaze for a few seconds, sensing the underlying sarcasm. They were like two peas in a pod and didn't even realize it. Señora Morales turned to María and said, "I sent my son yesterday to try on the outfits, and he came back late. I trust there isn't a problem with the order. We have a deadline we must meet."

María's face reflected her nervousness. "I'm sure they will be completed in time, Señora."

María could feel Abuela's stare but refused to make eye contact. Abuela most likely figured out that Antonio was the boy she was with on the steps of the church the day before. She could almost hear the thoughts going through Abuela's mind.

"Where is your son?" Abuela asked. Now the color left María's face completely, shocked that Abuela would ask for Antonio.

"Antonio is walking around. I think he's hoping he sees his amigos here." Señora Morales was oblivious to the fact that María was probably the very friend Antonio was looking for.

Feeling the tension building, Magdalena broke the silence. "We still have the exhibits on the other side, Abuela."

"Yes! We should go see them," María said, anxiously tugging on Abuela's arm.

"Very well. It was nice to meet you all," Abuela said with a simple nod to Señora Morales.

As they walked away, María felt her heart continue to beat hard and fast. *What's wrong with me?* She didn't understand why she had all these mixed feelings. Why did the Morales family make her feel so nervous and paranoid? Not to mention the mere thought of Antonio made her have butterflies in her stomach and turn her personal climate similar to that of the equator. He was just a boy—a client of Sol y Luna. Her focus was on entering the convent in September, wasn't it?

"Don't you hear me talking to you," Olga shouted, startling María.

"What? I didn't hear you," María replied.

"You need to stop daydreaming and pay attention," Olga said while she motioned to the exhibits.

"What is it, Olga?" María said, aggravated at Olga's attitude.

"Abuela is at the ceramics booth over there. She bumped into your client lady again, and it looks like her son is with her this time."

María stood frozen, afraid to turn around and see if it was truly Antonio talking with Abuela. All she could think of to do was play it off like she didn't care. Maybe if she acted nonchalantly, Olga and Abuela would stop trying to uncover something that didn't exist.

María turned around and confirmed her fears. "Oh yes, that's him," María said. Trying to shift the focus, she said, "Can we go now? My feet really hurt in these sandals."

"Let me find Magdalena. You go get Abuela," Olga paused, expecting a reaction from María.

"Fine. I'll go get Abuela and meet you at the exit," María said calmly, though beads of sweat started to form on her forehead. María walked toward the booth with a serious look, determined to mask the anxiety she felt.

"Ria!" The little boy yelled when he saw her. María simply touched his head and looked at Abuela.

"Olga is getting Lena so we can leave now. My sandals are hurting my feet."

"María, don't be so rude. Aren't you going to say hello to Antonio Morales?" Abuela said in a sly tone.

"Of course, I'm sorry. Hello Antonio," María said looking everywhere but at Antonio. "Abuela, we have to go. It's going to rain."

"I thought your feet hurt," Abuela said with a chuckle. "Now it's the weather? Which one is it?"

María looked at Abuela hard as if to telepathically send her a message that she was not amused by her sarcasm. Just then, Olga and Magdalena walked up, ready to leave.

"Ok, ok," Abuela conceded. "It looks like we are ready to go home. Adios."

Embarrassed by the whole exchange with Abuela, María was already walking toward the exit of the festival while the others were still saying their goodbyes to the Morales family.

Soon everyone caught up to María, and they walked up Cocquina Street in silence. María just wanted to get home so she could spend some time alone and pray. She planned to recite the Rosary in hopes that she would feel better afterward.

"María," Abuela started. "Why are you so quiet? Is there something that I need to know?"

"My feet hurt, Abuela. That is all there is to know."

"María," Abuela replied in a higher tone. Suddenly it started to rain, and María couldn't help but smile. It was like answered prayer.

"I can't talk now, Abuela. We have to run. Rain!"

Chapter 4

María spent the next two weeks putting in extra hours at Sol y Luna and volunteering at the convent. She did everything to stay focused and not give anyone reason to question her priorities. The nuns were impressed with her acts of service and were confident that they made the right decision in accepting her into the program for the fall. At the same time, Señora Medina was dreading the day she would have to say goodbye to her young protégé. Sol y Luna would miss a very talented seamstress.

With all of the recent distractions, María had no time to let her mind wander about Antonio. Abuela seemed to have forgotten as well; she never brought him up.

Señora Morales was scheduled to pick up the order in another week. After that, María was sure she wouldn't see the Morales family ever again. The thought of that gave her peace. She hated not having control of her emotions, and the Moraleses brought out a spectrum of emotions in María.

Saturday morning, María woke up as she normally did, listening to the birds sing while she prayed. María was working a full day at Sol y Luna, and then she had prayer service at the church afterward. María wore a modest dress that would suit the long day out of the house. She was looking forward to having the next four days off from Sol y Luna and the convent. Even though María had a goal to make as much money this summer to pay for school next year, she wanted to enjoy at least a few days of her summer before school started again.

María arrived at Sol y Luna at 10 am. Señora Medina had her working in the back all day on uniforms. Usually, María worked in the store on Saturdays, but Señora Media was working on a deadline for the department store. The day went by fast. María was able to sew three jumpers during her time in the back. It was fun working with the other seamstresses there.

Señora Media had purchased a radio so they could listen to their novellas. Some of those stories made María laugh, but most of them left her wanting. María would daydream about her life if she didn't go to the convent. She fantasized about being a fashion designer and living in the city with a handsome boyfriend, just like Meliza Cruz, the main character in the novella.

At three o'clock, María started to clean up her station to get ready to leave for the day. She heard the bell ring in the front and the sound of a loud familiar voice. *It couldn't be,* she thought to herself. María walked closer to the curtain to hear the voice better.

Suddenly, Señora Medina came rushing through. "I need the Morales order!" Just before the curtains closed, María caught a glimpse of Antonio's profile.

"I thought they weren't due for another week," María said, confused.

"I called them last night and told them they could pick up today. I did the finishing touches myself to help

Ramón get this order off his list." Señora Medina placed the freshly pressed garments on a rack to wheel out to the front.

"But Ramón is not here to see if any adjustments need to be made," María said apprehensively.

"María," Señora Medina stopped, slightly annoyed. "They took care of that at the last fitting. What's wrong with you?"

"Oh, nothing," María said with a nervous chuckle. "It's just that I know how difficult Señora Morales can be. I wanted to make sure everything was perfect so you didn't have to see her ugly side."

"It's ok, niña. These garments are perfect. Now come and help me package them." Señora Medina started to wheel the rack to the front of the store, expecting María to follow. "Vamos!" Señora Medina ordered as she entered the front store.

María took a deep breath and said to herself, "You can do this."

When María walked through the curtains, Señora Morales was already inspecting the garments one by one.

"These came out really nice, Estela," Señora Morales said without looking up. "Luckily for you, you won't have to see my ugly side, right, María?"

"Señora Morales, I . . . I didn't mean . . ." María started to explain but stopped when the woman raised her hand in an effort to silence her.

"How much do I owe?" Señora Morales asked as she walked over to the counter to settle the bill with Señora Medina.

María started to bag the garments when Antonio stood close to her and whispered, "I'm sorry." María continued to place the plastic bags over each garment, ignoring Antonio completely.

"María, please accept my apologies," he tried again. María looked back to make sure the ladies were pre-occupied and responded to Antonio in a harsh tone. "You seem to always be apologizing, and you seem to think I care."

María walked away to find more garment bags, leaving Antonio feeling guilty. Señora Morales finished paying her balance and started to grab some of the bags to put them in her car.

"Antonio, you grab the rest," she yelled as she walked out. "Gracias, Estela!"

Señora Medina went to the back room to put the money in the safe. Realizing she was alone with Antonio in the store, María's heart started to beat fast.

"María, I didn't mean to hurt you by walking away," Antonio started quickly, taking advantage of the short moment they had alone. "I didn't want to get you into any more trouble."

"It's fine. All is well," María said. "Here are your garments, Mr. Morales. Thank you for shopping at Sol y Luna." She handed him the last of the bags and walked away.

Just then, the front door opened, and Señora Morales stood in the doorway saying, "Hurry up, Antonio. I have to get back home!"

Antonio gave María one last look and said, "Gracias, Señorita," and walked out the door. María wanted to cry. Why did this boy stir up these feelings in her? María didn't know that Señora Medina was standing by the curtains and witnessed the last exchange.

"Are you ok, María?"

"Señora Medina, you startled me!"

Señora Medina walked over to María and gave her a hug. "María, stay focused, ok?"

"Si, Señora," she replied. Now that the Morales family was out of her life, staying focused would not be a problem.

María gathered her belongings and said her goodbyes. Although she was physically and emotionally tired, she would go to afternoon prayer at the church anyway. After walking one block, María saw Antonio standing against a Pontiac.

"What are you doing here?" María asked. "The owner of that car won't be happy that you're leaning against it."

"He doesn't mind," Antonio said with a smile.

"Really. And how do you know this?" María asked, crossing her arms.

"Because it's *my* car," Antonio said, laughing. María's eyes opened wide.

"You have your own car?" María walked around the car to see it in all angles.

"My father bought it for me two weeks ago," Antonio said, amazed at María's enthusiasm for the car. "Let's go for a drive," he suggested. María entertained the idea, excited at the thought of being in a car. There were only two times that María had been in a car, and both times, she was too young to remember the experience. "Come," Antonio said as he opened the car door. María completely forgot she was on her way to church. All she could think of was taking a quick ride in a car around the block. Without saying a word, María stepped into the car.

Antonio drove cautiously down the road in silence. María tried not to make it obvious how impressed she was with his driving. Every time Antonio turned to look at her, she pretended to look out the window. After a few minutes, María realized they were farther than just around the block.

"Where are we going?" María asked with sudden fear in her voice.

Antonio turned to María and simply said, "Trust me."

Something in the way he looked at her made María feel that she could trust him. Before she knew it, they were at the beach. María had lived life confined to the small perimeter that included school, work, church, and home. She had never traveled the distance to the beach that was only thirty minutes away by car. María couldn't contain her excitement. Antonio opened the door for her, and she stepped out of the car, overwhelmed by the vast body of water.

"Antonio, how did you know?" María said softly. "How did you know that I would like this?" Antonio shrugged his shoulders and looked around.

"I had a feeling. We are so much alike in other ways. I love the beach, so I figured you would probably love it too." Antonio reached for her hand.

María didn't hesitate and joined hands with him as he walked her to the shore. It was a beautiful summer evening, but María noticed no one was on the beach.

"Where is everyone? Why isn't the beach full of people?" María asked, soaking in her surroundings.

"This is a private beach. My mother cleans for many of the families around here. She says that a lot of them go on vacation elsewhere for the summer." Antonio still held onto María's hand now with his eyes focused on her.

"If I lived here," María said, "I wouldn't ever leave. It's so beautiful.

"Have you ever seen the sunrise from here?" Antonio asked with excitement in his voice. "It's even more beautiful."

María watched Antonio speak with sincere admiration for creation. It wasn't every day you meet a teenaged boy that spoke so passionately about nature's beauty.

Suddenly, María became aware of the time. "I have to get back! Please take me back now," María shouted, trying to quickly walk on the dry sand. Antonio took long strides to keep up with her. Soon they were back on the road.

Remembering the episode with Señora Reyes, María asked Antonio to drop her off on another street by her house, and she would walk the rest of the way. There was nothing on that block but a tavern. If anyone saw her on that dead-end street, she was sure they wouldn't say a word to Abuela. They would have to admit they were at the bar, and that would be scandalous enough. Her secret was safe.

When they reached the drop off spot, Antonio turned the car off and stared at the wheel. "What's wrong?" María asked.

Antonio looked sad and hopeless. "I really like spending time with you, María." Still staring at the wheel, Antonio continued, "I just really hate saying goodbye."

María smiled. His transparency was endearing. "Well, we won't say goodbye then," María replied. "Let's just say, *until next time.*"

"How about tomorrow," Antonio quickly responded, making eye contact. "Let me show you the sunrise at the beach tomorrow." María let out a big sigh, knowing Abuela would never allow her to go on this harmless adventure. "Please, María," Antonio pleaded as he took María's hand with both of his. María couldn't bring herself to say no.

"I'll meet you here before the rooster crows." Antonio's heart leaped with excitement at María's response.

"Gracias!" he said with his infamous smile.

"Until next time," María said as she stepped out of the car. Antonio followed her discreetly as she walked home the half mile. All the way home, María thought about how she would explain being home late. She rehearsed different ways of how she would explain her joy ride with Antonio.

As María got closer to the house, she noticed a car driving away. Her stomach turned at the thought that it may have been another informant. How would she get out of this one? María looked behind her just as Antonio was making a turn to head home. She smiled as he drove away. It was sweet of him to follow her home safely. Too bad, after tonight, she may never see him again.

María took a deep breath and prepared herself for the worst. There was a lot of commotion going on in the house that she could hear it from outside. María was certain it was Abuela planning out her punishment for being with a boy at the beach. When she opened the back door, Abuela, Olga, and Magdalena were in the kitchen talking all at the same time.

"What's going on?" María asked hesitantly.

"María!" Abuela shouted. "Come over here." María feared for her life and looked to her sisters for help. It was then she noticed that they were smiling—big smiles. María looked at Abuela again, and she saw Abuela was smiling too. She took slow steps toward her grandmother, afraid of what she had walked into.

"We just had a visitor," Abuela started. "Senor Guzman just stopped by with some news."

"Who is Senor Guzman?" María asked, afraid of the answer.

"Senor Guzman is an administrator from the hospital. He was impressed by Olga's volunteer work there last spring that he recommended her for the nursing program at the college in the city." Abuela sat down to catch her breath.

"That's great news, Olga," María responded with a hint of relief. She was not the focus of the evening excitement. Abuela lifted her hand to stop María from talking.

"That's not all, María. Senor Guzman stopped by to say that the college accepted her into the program with a scholarship! Olga is going to the city in September for nursing school. Gloria a Dios!"

"Congratulations, Hermana! This is what you prayed for," María said as she embraced her sister.

"And the best news of all," Magdalena interrupted, "I get to have the room all to myself!" Everyone broke into laughter, and the excitement started all over again with everyone talking at the same time. María couldn't remember a time when Olga looked so happy. This was truly a blessing.

María was so caught up in the news that she forgot all about her afternoon excursion and her early morning plans with Antonio. It wasn't until she was in bed later that night, minutes away from sleep, did she remember her appointment the next morning. She was even more excited to see him now so she could share the family's good news with her friend. After all, he *was* just a friend.

Chapter 5

María could barely sleep, waking up every thirty minutes to check the clock. She didn't want to be late meeting Antonio on Calle Palmas. She could hear Abuela snoring loudly in her bedroom. As long as the rumbling sound continued, María could sneak out successfully. Even though she technically wasn't doing anything wrong, María knew Abuela would think the worst and make an exaggerated display of it if she got caught.

Just before dawn, María slowly made her track down the street. It was very quiet, with not a person in sight. Suddenly María was aware of what she was doing and the dangers of walking in the streets in the dark. Fear overcame her when she heard footsteps behind her. Too afraid to turn around, María started to walk faster. Why didn't she tell Antonio to just pick her up at the house? The footsteps sounded quicker and heavier. María's heart started to beat fast as she nearly jogged to meet Antonio. She was almost to the meeting stop. Once she turned the corner of Calle Palmas, she was sure to lose whoever was behind her.

As soon as she turned the corner, María's eyes searched for Antonio and his car. She walked frantically, eyes wide open, trying to see a sign of her friend waiting for her. Was she too early? María started to say a Hail Mary under her breath when she realized Antonio wasn't there. She put herself in a situation where a number of things could happen to her, and she had no one else to blame.

María stopped suddenly and tried to catch her breath. In an act of surrender, María slowly turned around to see if she was still being followed.

"Antonio!" she screamed. "It was you the whole time?"

Antonio chuckled. "Who did you think it was?"

María's fear turned into anger. "You think this is funny? I thought you were a street thug!" María hit Antonio in the arm. "I was afraid!"

Antonio quickly grasped that this was no laughing matter. "María, I'm sorry," he explained. "But did you really think I was going to let you walk all that way alone in the dark?"

María's face began to relax when Antonio's true motives were realized. She just looked at him, embarrassed for getting angry when he was only looking out for her well-being.

"We have to go," Antonio said as he walked back three cars away. He opened the car door for María, and she quietly stepped in. It was like déjà vu. The drive to the beach was silent. Antonio felt bad for upsetting María, and María felt bad for overreacting.

When they arrived at the beach, Antonio continued to play the gentleman and opened the car door for María. He reached in the back seat for a blanket, grabbed her hand, and they walked to the ideal spot. Antonio opened the blanket on the sand and motioned for María to sit. Once they were both sitting on the blanket, Antonio pointed toward the sea. They were just in time. A light started to peak over the water painting a beautiful hue in the sky.

María held a hand to her mouth in awe. She had never experienced the sunrise. Even though she woke up early every morning to pray, she never paid attention to how the sunlight chased away the darkness in such a beautiful way. They both sat in silence watching the sun rise. After a while, María stood up and walked toward the shore. Antonio didn't know María was crying and that she was trying to hide her tears from him.

When the sun was almost completely up, Antonio walked over to join María by the shore. María quickly wiped her face so he wouldn't see her tears. Antonio put his hand on the small of María's back, and she jumped. His touch was like electricity to her. Antonio looked at her, puzzled by her reaction. María could feel her cheeks get warm, embarrassed again by her actions. She took a step closer back toward Antonio. He put his hand on her back again, but this time, he drew her into an embrace. María was shocked by his boldness but liked it. Gradually she raised her arms and hugged him back.

When María tried to pull away after a few seconds, Antonio held on tighter. María felt powerless in Antonio's arms. She could feel his heartbeat, which made her butterflies make a comeback.

When Antonio released his hold on María, he looked at her in the eyes and broke the silence for the first time in an hour. "I'm never going to hurt you. Don't fear me." Antonio reached for her hand, and they started their walk back to the car.

María stopped short and turned toward Antonio. "I'm sorry," she started. "I'm sorry for yelling at you earlier and hitting you. This morning was amazing. I have never seen something so beautiful, and I am grateful for the experience."

Antonio interrupted, "We can do it again, anytime you want—"

"Let me finish, Antonio," María continued, now standing confidently. "I am grateful, but we cannot see each other again."

Antonio opened his mouth to speak, but María held her hand to it.

"I don't like these feelings I am having, Antonio. They scare me. I am going to Altagracia Prep in September, and you are going to college. Our friendship will end eventually. It might as well end now before we go any further."

Predictably, the look on Antonio's face changed. It was his turn to be angry. He let go of María's hand and swiftly walked again to the car. When they reached the car, he turned to María, who was ready for his rebuttal. "I have never met a more beautiful person inside and out. I like our friendship, and I like the idea of being better friends. If all we have is this summer, why spend it apart and miserable? Please, María," Antonio pleaded.

María opened the car door and simply replied, "We have to go."

Driving back seemed to take longer than it did before. María hated all of these emotions she felt. Instead of going home, she asked Antonio to drop her off at the church. She needed to pray. Antonio pulled in o the empty lot behind the church as requested.

Just as María touched the door handle, Antonio made his final appeal. "Please, María. There is a new movie at the Riviera tonight. Meet me there."

María opened the door and stepped out of the car without responding. As she walked around to the front of the church, she could hear Antonio's words ringing in her ears over and over again.

María made it inside the empty church and sat midway through. "What am I doing?" she asked herself.

Don't awaken love, she heard in response. It was at that moment she understood what Ramón was trying to tell her. "Don't awaken love," María repeated to herself out aloud.

"What did you say?"

María looked up and saw Sister Rebeca standing in front of her holding a stack of prayer books.

"Oh, Sister Rebeca, I'm sorry I didn't see you standing there." Sister Rebeca was one of the nuns who taught at Altagracia Prep. She was one of the youngest teachers and also María's favorite.

"Are you ok, María? You don't look yourself," Sister Rebeca asked.

"I'm fine, Sister. What are those books?" María asked in an effort to shift the focus from her.

"I came to pick up some prayer books from the church to use for my summer theology class," Sister Rebeca replied as she sat down next to María. "You know," she continued, "I remember when I was in your shoes, waiting for my life to start. The summer before prep school was the most exhilarating time of my life. I remember going on vacation with my family to Estados Unidos. We had so much fun in Florida. We stayed with my Tio Eli and his family for three weeks. They had a big house with a pool where I learned how to swim. We ate amazing meals all day long every day. I didn't want to leave!"

María giggled at Sister Rebeca, imagining her as a young teenager having fun on vacation.

"No, I'm serious," Sister Rebeca said in a different tone. "I did not want to leave Florida. I wanted to stay with my uncle and enjoy the sweet life I believed they had. I didn't want to go to Altagracia Prep anymore or be a nun, for that matter. I wanted to be a model. In three short weeks, I wanted to turn my back on everything I knew to be true and take a different path than the one God had for me."

"Sister Rebeca, I had no idea," María said, fascinated by the insight on this nun's past. "Thank goodness you didn't follow through, or we wouldn't have you with us today," María said with a big smile.

"Yes, María, but it almost didn't turn out that way," Sister Rebeca continued. "Sometimes we look at things people have and think we are missing out on something when what we have is just as good or even better." Sister Rebeca placed her had on María's. "When you know that God has a plan for you, you don't go searching for other options. God's plan is always best." Sister Rebeca looked intensely at María for a moment, searching for a sign that she understood the message she was trying to deliver, but María didn't blink.

"Do you remember the story in the Bible about Jesus walking on water, María?"

"Of course, I do. It is one of my favorites of all the amazing things Jesus did," María answered with light in her eyes.

"María, that story is not a report of how Jesus pulled off another trick. It is about who we are and what we can be when we trust Him and focus on Him." Sister Rebeca paused, waiting for a response from María but was disappointed yet again. "When Peter was focused on Jesus and put all his faith in Him, Jesus called for him, and Peter was able to walk on water. The minute Peter looked away and took his eyes off of Jesus, he started to question what he was doing, and he sank. You have been called, María. Don't take your eyes off of Him."

Suddenly aware of what Sister Rebeca was saying to her, María nodded in agreement.

"Well, I have to get back to the convent," Sister Rebeca said as she stood up. "Remember, if you need to talk about anything, you know where to find me."

"Thank you, Sister. I will remember that," María responded.

As Sister Rebeca gathered her books to go, she whispered to María, "And if you need a ride to church, I can take you in *my* car." María gasped, realizing that Sister Rebeca must have seen her get out of Antonio's car. Embarrassed by the perception Sister Rebeca probably had of her, María was speechless.

An hour went by after Sister Rebeca left, and María just sat in the church thinking about what her mentor said. She had to stay focused. She had nine weeks before going to Altagracia, and she needed to stay focused on that and nothing else.

When María finally made it home, it was nearly lunchtime. Abuela was sitting in the kitchen drinking coffee with Señora Medina.

"Señora Medina," María said, surprised to see her. "What are you doing here?"

"That's rude, María!" Abuela snapped.

"I'm sorry. I didn't mean it that way," María apologized. "I meant, is something wrong at the shop?"

"Everything is fine, María," Señora Media replied. "I just stopped by to give you a little token of my appreciation." She handed María an envelope. "You have been working very hard the past couple of weeks at Sol y Luna, and I wanted you to know how grateful I am."

María was so excited to receive the gift. She quickly opened the envelope to reveal its contents. When she discovered what the gift was, her big smile quickly faded.

"What is it, María?" Abuela asked.

"I got her tickets for all of you to go to the cinema tonight," Señora Media answered with excitement. "Tonight they are showing the American movie *The 10 Commandments*. I've heard about it from my friends in Estados Unidos. You're going to love it!"

"Oh Estela, that is so gracious of you," Abuela responded, elated by the gift. "María, tell Señora Medina how grateful you are." María was paralyzed by the irony in the gift. Antonio had invited her to the cinema, and she already decided not to go and keep a distance from him. Was it a coincidence that she now received tickets from Señora Medina or the same exact movie on the same exact evening?

"María!" Abuela shouted.

"Señora Medina, muchas gracias," María responded.

"You almost had her speechless, Estela!" Abuela teased. She had no idea why María was at a loss for words.

"I must go back to the shop now," Señora Medina said. "Enjoy your days off, and enjoy the cinema tonight. Adios!" Señora Medina was out the door in a flash in her usual hurried style.

"Girls," Abuela shouted. "We're going to the Riviera tonight!" Abuela was so excited, and soon Magdalena and Olga joined in on the excitement as she filled them in.

"Oh María," Magdalena said. "Tonight is going to be the best!" María smiled at her little sister, but deep inside, she was scared of what the night would bring. She didn't trust her heart when Antonio was around, and seeing him again would only make her even more confused about her feelings.

"Yes, Lena. The best night."

Chapter 6

When the Riviera opened up in town six months prior, it was all people could talk about. María remembered Ramón talking about going there the first week it opened. "It is an impressive theater," he said, "but it brings out the town snobs." Ramón swore he wouldn't go again because it was too expensive and was more of a place where socialites frequented. Ramón wasn't a fan of the socialites.

Tonight, María and her family would be among *those* people. She had butterflies in her stomach from the excitement. She didn't know what to expect from the night between the magnificent theater and Antonio being there. Either way, she would try to play it cool and not get anxious by it all.

"Honestly, María, I don't understand how you have these moments where you turn off the world," Olga said, annoyed at María.

"What?" María responded, lost by the comment.

"I've been talking to you for five minutes, and you've been in a daze staring at the wall. Did you even hear what I said?" Olga snapped.

"She's daydreaming about tonight, Olga," Magdalena interrupted, defending her older sister like she usually does. "This is the last exciting thing she'll experience before going to the convent."

"That's not true!" María shouted. "My life will be full of excitement. Just because I am going to Altagracia doesn't mean I'm going to stop living!"

"María, I didn't mean it like that," Magdalena replied with tears in her eyes. "I only meant that you probably wouldn't have opportunities like this because . . ."

"Leave it alone, Magdalena," Olga barked. "Just leave her alone."

"Well, I'm sorry," Magdalena whispered, making a final attempt at an apology.

"It's ok, Lena," María said. "I'm sorry I yelled."

"Can I go back to what I was saying?" Olga shouted. "Abuela said we need to be ready in fifteen minutes. Remember, we are walking there."

"What?" María stood up, bewildered. "I thought for sure Abuela would have hired a driver to take us. That is a six-mile walk in fancy shoes!"

"As I was explaining when you were ignoring me," Olga continued, "Abuela said to wear your walking shoes. She will put everyone's fancy shoes in a bag. When we get close to the theater, we can change shoes." María gave a sigh of relief. She didn't understand Abuela's stubbornness about automobiles. She never liked to ride in them.

María quickly put on her dress after trying on four others. She decided on a black and white polka dot dress with a white sweater to drape over her shoulders. It was one of the first dresses she made but never had an opportunity to wear it. *This will have to do*, she thought.

The Garcia women made their way to the theater, and the weather was in their favor. Magdalena talked the entire time about everything. María didn't mind. It made the long walk more entertaining. Before they knew it, they were one block away from the theater.

"Alright, girls, switch out your shoes," Abuela said as she passed out the shoes. María started to take her shoes off in an effort to make the switch quickly without being noticed. As she balanced on one foot to put her formal shoe on, a car slowly drove by, and all María could hear was laughter. When she looked up, she saw it was Señora Morales. María could feel the blood leaving her face. She wanted to turn around and run back home.

"That woman is unbelievable," Abuela said through clenched teeth as she watched the car drive away.

María stood there with her head down, hiding her embarrassment while the others switched out their shoes, unmoved by what had happened.

Abuela realized María wasn't putting her shoes on, and her face revealed another level of anger. "María, don't tell me that you are going to let that woman ruin your night."

Head still hung low, María did not respond. Abuela stared at her granddaughter, realizing that although María was mature for her age, she was still a teenager. Her face relaxed, and her tone softened. "María, if you are so embarrassed and ashamed of who you are, then you are ashamed of the God who made you."

"Oh no, Abuela," María responded quickly. "I am not ashamed of my God. I would never be ashamed of Him!" María bent down to change her shoes. When she stood up, Abuela was still staring at her. There was love in her eyes, but she didn't say a word. Abuela rarely ever expressed affection toward María, even when the moment called for it.

"Can we go now?" Magdalena said, anxious to get to the theater.

They quickly walked the last block to the Riviera. There was a big crowd of people in line to buy tickets to see the American movie. María walked right up to the usher at the door and handed him the tickets, and he responded with a nod for them to go inside.

As they made their way inside, María saw Señora Morales standing in the long line waiting to buy a ticket. María made contact with her and smiled. "Vindication," she whispered to herself.

Ushers escorted the women into the main theater and directed them to sit wherever they wanted in the premium section. The movie would begin in a few minutes, and the seats were filling fast. María couldn't help but nervously search the crowd for Antonio. *Guess he didn't come.*

Suddenly the lights dimmed, and the movie's opening credits began. Magdalena squeezed María's arm from sheer excitement. María turned her head one last time toward the entrance when she saw an usher with a flashlight escorting a group of teens to a row of seats. María's insides leaped when she saw Antonio in the group. Oblivious to her, Antonio followed the group and sat in the assigned seat. María turned her focus back to the large screen.

The story of Moses brought to life in such an epic way was amazing to this small town girl. When intermission came, María did not want to get up for fear of missing any part of the movie when it started again.

Olga and Abuela went to the restrooms while Lena went to get refreshments for everyone at the concessions counter. María sat in the theater and watched people engage in enthusiastic commentary about the film. She scanned the theater looking to see where Antonio disappeared when she spotted an old friend.

"Ana!" María called out. Her childhood friend quickly walked up the aisle in her form-fitting dress.

"María, what are you doing here?" Ana asked loudly, causing people to turn their heads. They hadn't seen each other since Ana's family moved to the city two years ago. Although Ana was only a few months older than María, she had the figure of a full-grown woman. María looked at Ana from head to toe, noticing her dress that accentuated every curve.

"Ana, look at you," María said with a hint of envy. "You look like a fashion model!"

"That's because I am," Ana responded with a giggle. "Mami paid for me to go to modeling school last summer, and I have had some great opportunities ever since." María was so caught up in what Ana was saying that she didn't notice that Antonio had walked up behind her.

"Well, who is this?" Ana asked in a sensual tone. María was caught off-guard when she saw Antonio standing next to her.

"My name is Antonio Morales. I am María's friend." When he extended his hand, Ana grabbed it and pulled Antonio close and kissed him on the cheek.

"Any friend of María's is a friend of mine," Ana responded. María felt warmth make its way to her face. Watching how Ana flirted with Antonio and how he enjoyed it brought emotions she had never felt before. The two talked while María watched as if she was a spectator at a tennis match. They forgot she was even there.

The theater lights flickered to signify that the movie would begin in two minutes. María looked back to her seats and saw that Abuela and her sisters had returned. "I'm going to sit down," María said, interrupting the love connection. Barely acknowledging her existence, Ana waved, "Bye, Ria," without taking her eyes off of Antonio.

María settled back into her seat quietly. "Is that Ana talking to that horrible lady's son?" Abuela asked.

"Sí," María gave a short response, pretending not to care. The lights dimmed, and the movie began again. María could see shadows of people going to their seats. She tried hard to focus on the movie, but her mind kept wandering to Antonio and Ana. *Was he interested in Ana?* She thought to herself. Ana acted so sophisticated, and Antonio was clearly drawn to her. María's jealousy grew as different scenarios played in her head. *They will probably get married. I'm sure they will have a lot of children.*

Suddenly Abuela shouted, "Gloria a Dios!" And the crowd followed with a mixture of applauds and gasps.

"What's wrong?" María said to Magdalena, startled.

"Moses split the Red Sea!" Magdalena whispered, sitting at the edge of her seat. "Pay attention!"

María felt a wave of sudden guilt. They were blessed to see one of the most epic films about a biblical event in a beautiful theater, and she was wasting it thinking about a boy. To make it even worse, her little sister was the one to indirectly point it out to her.

The rest of the move didn't disappoint. It was just as amazing as the first half. When the lights turned on, people slowly gathered their belongings and exited the theater. María noticed that Ana sat next to Antonio for the second half of the movie. She pretended not to care as Magdalena nudged her to keep moving toward the aisle. When they reached outside in front of the theater, Abuela instructed them to use the restroom again before they started on their trek back home. María and Magdalena went back inside, leaving Abuela and Olga outside.

Abuela watched people walk out of the theater in their fancy outfits. Most of the patrons were unfamiliar to Abuela, and she knew mostly everyone in the small town except the wealthy people who loved by the beach. Ana walked out of the theater with Antonio and his friends, followed by Señora Morales and her sister. Olga spotted them right away.

"Abuela," she said.

"I see them," Abuela responded, narrowing her eyes on Señora Morales. When Ana saw Abuela, she ran up to her and greeted her with an embrace.

"Abuela, como están?" Ana asked. Abuela was pleased to see María's old friend but not pleased with the transformation.

"Niña, you've changed," Abuela said in a judging tone.

"I am modeling now," Ana responded. "I'm on my way to becoming rich and famous!" She greeted Olga with a kiss on the cheek. Olga was not impressed. She always thought that Ana was a conceited girl.

"I didn't know you knew the Morales family," Abuela questioned.

"Oh, I just met them today," Ana responded, waving Antonio over to them. "They are nice people." Abuela gestured for Ana to stop, but before she knew it, she was standing face to face with Señora Morales.

"Señora Garcia," Señora Morales said with a nod toward Abuela. She replied with a simple nod and didn't say a word. Antonio extended a hand to Abuela and Olga and greeted them.

"Where is María?" he asked.

"She and Magdalena went to the restroom," Olga answered. "As soon as they return, we will be on our way."

"I will be happy to give you all a ride home," Antonio offered. "I can fit everyone in my car."

"No," Abuela snapped, barely giving Antonio a chance to finish his sentence. "We are fine walking."

"There she is!" Ana said, pointing at María and Magdalena exiting the theater. She ran and gave Magdalena a tight hug. "Look at you, Lena! You're growing up so fast!" María couldn't hide her nervousness. *Why were the Moraleses always around?* She said her hellos to everyone and tried not to make eye contact with Antonio until he addressed her in front of everyone.

"María, I was telling your grandmother that I have a car, and I could give you all a ride home."

"Oh, Abuela, that's a fantastic idea," Magdalena shouted.

"Mr. Morales," Abuela said in a low voice, "As I said before, we will walk. But thank you for the offer." She picked up the bag with the shoes and said, "Good night everyone. Let's go, girls." Olga followed Abuela briskly down the street. Magdalena locked arms with María and said, "We better go." María shook her head and smiled in agreement.

"Antonio," Señora Morales said, "How rude of you not to ask Ana if she needed a ride home." Antonio looked at María as if he were waiting for approval.

"I would love a ride to my uncle's house," Ana replied. "I think my cousins left me already anyway.

"Good," Señora Morales said. "It's all settled then. Antonio, you take Ana home. Such a beautiful girl like you shouldn't be on the streets walking home." Magdalena tugged at María's arm again, confirming that they had stayed longer than they should have. They turned and hurriedly walked down the street to catch up with Abuela and Olga.

"Are you ok, María?" Magdalena whispered as they got closer to the others.

"I'm fine, Lena," she responded, still arm in arm with her sister.

As usual, Magdalena talked most of the way home. A block away from the house, María noticed a familiar car following them. She couldn't help but smile when she realized it was Antonio. Keeping her discovery to herself, she continued walking toward the house.

"Finally, we made it!" Magdalena shouted when they reached the front door. When they entered the house, Abuela said goodnight and went straight to her room and closed the door. Olga and Magdalena went to their room.

"Aren't you coming?" Olga asked. María quickly thought of a lie.

"I'll be in soon. I'm going to sit out back for some quiet time. I'll be in soon." Olga looked at her hard, knowing it was a lie but too tired to challenge her sister to find out what she was up to. When María heard the bedroom door shut, she swiftly went out the back door. Just as she expected, Antonio was there leaning against his car, waiting for her.

"How did you know I would come outside?" María asked, slightly perturbed that he knew her so well.

"I took a chance," Antonio responded, flashing his handsome smile.

"Where is Ana?" María asked, crossing her arms. "I thought surely you would still be with her."

"How can I be with her when I can't stop thinking about you?" Antonio confessed as he walked toward María until they were inches apart. Holding her gaze, Antonio unfolded María's arms and pulled her in for an embrace. María didn't know what to do. She liked being in his arms, but she knew it wasn't right. When she started to pull away, Antonio pulled her again, but this time, he kissed María on the cheek.

"I like you, María," Antonio said.

"I know you do," María responded. "I like you too. But we can't like each other!"

Antonio looked at her and whispered, "Let's go for a quick drive."

"You know I can't," María retorted. "It's late, and my sisters are probably wondering where I am."

"I just want to spend some time with you, María. Let's go," Antonio pleaded. María didn't feel like arguing. Her flesh was winning, and she didn't want to fight anymore. Antonio opened the car door to see if María would accept the invitation. With a slight smile, María climbed into the car.

Being that it was late at night, there weren't a lot of cars on the road. Antonio arrived at the beach fairly quickly.

"It's so breezy out here. It feels really nice by the water," María said nervously.

"Do you need me to get you a jacket?" Antonio asked, just as nervous. "I have one in the trunk."

"No, I'm fine," María said rubbing her arms. "This is beautiful, but it's late, and I don't want Abuela to find out that I am gone." Antonio straightened, as if a surge of boldness came through him.

"María, we may never have this opportunity again. Can't we just enjoy this time together?" María knew he was right. After today, they would only have a little over a month before they went to school, and María planned to spend all of that time working and preparing for Altagracia.

Antonio found a spot on the beach and opened up a blanket they could sit on. María was still in her polka dot dress and was nervous about getting it dirty.

"I'm glad you brought the blanket," María sighed. As the two of them sat and watched the beach waves, Antonio started to open up his heart to María.

"I think about you all the time—" María opened her mouth to interrupt, and Antonio stopped her. "Let me finish. It's my turn to talk." He started to tell her about the things he wanted in life, about going to college and becoming a lawyer, getting married, and having a family. He talked about being an only child and how he wanted to have several children because he didn't want any of them to feel alone like he did growing up. He spoke about wanting to teach his children responsibility. Although he loved his parents and appreciated everything they did for him, he recognized that he rarely had to work for anything.

As Antonio spoke transparently, María realized how deep her feelings were for him. It was also the first time thoughts of Altagracia and the convent didn't cross her mind. María held Antonio's hand to show that he had her attention. The more he talked, the more she wanted to know.

"Will you wait for me?" Antonio asked.

"Wait for you?" María asked, confused. "What do you mean?"

"I know your place in my life. I may be only eighteen years old, but I know that you are part of my future. I've shared all of this with you because I know that you will be mine forever." Antonio studied María's face for a reaction. "God brought you into my life for a reason."

María's eyes opened wide. No one had ever spoken to her like that before. Her afternoon novellas were the closest she had ever gotten to an example of love. Here she was, sitting on the beach in a romantic setting with a handsome college boy. It was almost like a scene from the novellas themselves.

"Antonio, how can I wait for you when I'm going to be a nun?" María replied, remembering her commitment for the first time that night.

"Are you sure that is your destiny?" Antonio questioned. "Are you sure that is what God wants from you?"

"It's . . . yes . . . it's something that I've wanted since I was a little girl," María managed to respond.

"You are no longer a little girl, María. Your little girl dreams are not the same as a woman's dreams." Antonio knew exactly the right words to use to get María's attention.

He sees me as a woman.

"What about Ana?" María asked in a jealous tone. "I saw the way you looked at her. Are you sure *she's* not the woman in your future?" Antonio looked at María, surprised by her question after everything he shared with her. He leaned in slowly and kissed María on the lips. Startled by his actions and her body's reaction, María put her fingers on her forbidden lips.

Antonio pulled María's hand down from her lips and kissed her again, but this time with passion. María didn't know what to do, but this time, she didn't pull away, and she kissed him back.

Stopping to catch a breath, Antonio looked at María surprisingly. "You've kissed before," he said.

"No!" María quickly responded. "I've never kissed a boy before . . . ever." Blushing, she looked down at her hands. "You are my first kiss."

"It's as if your lips were made for mine," Antonio said with intensity in his eyes. Forgetting who she was and where she was, María let Antonio kiss her again without resistance. He slowly guided her down on the blanket. Touching her body, Antonio brought fear and intrigue to María at the same time. Losing control of herself, she took pleasure in being desired by Antonio and the way her body responded to him. As his hand made its way up her thigh, María exhaled his name. "Antonio, wait."

"Please, María," Antonio begged as any other eighteen-year-old boy would in this situation. The sound of the waves crashing and the hum of the tropical breeze made María feel like she was in a dream. María looked deep into Antonio's dark eyes. There was something different, almost animalistic, that told her she didn't have much choice but to give in completely to him. Regardless, her flesh didn't want him to stop.

Moments later, the reality of what had just happened hit her. María was speechless. *What have I done*, she thought. It didn't take long for the voice of shame to whisper in her ear. **You are no longer pure.** Dazed, as if she had just awakened from a dream, María slowly stood up.

"My dress!" María screamed. Stains of blood marked her dress. Frantically she tried to rub the spot, hoping to erase the stain and what they had just done.

Antonio grabbed her hands, "It's going to be fine. Let's go." He led her back to the car. As they drove home, María kept replaying what had happened in her head. Shame covered her like a wool sweater.

"María, I love you," Antonio said, breaking the silence. "I hope you know that." María turned to look at him, still not able to find the words to express what she was feeling. What did this all mean for her future with the convent?

When they arrived at the Garcia house, Antonio turned off the headlights and the ignition so the car didn't wake up anyone in the neighborhood. "You will wait for me, right?" Antonio asked. María looked at him with the same blank look and didn't respond. She opened the door and slowly got out of the car, leaving Antonio behind without a goodbye.

Sneaking into the house, María went straight to the bathroom to work on the stained dress. Silent tears rolled down her face as she scrubbed the spot that was her sin. **You will never be forgiven.** When that voice spoke to her again, María covered her mouth and wept even more. How could she become a nun now after what she did with Antonio?

After hanging the dress to dry, María grabbed her rosary beads and sat outside on the porch to pray. With every bead, she recited a prayer, one after another. Hours had passed, and she continued to pray on every bead. As dawn approached, María's tears stopped, and a plan for her future was devised. She would attend Altagracia Preparatory School and complete secondary school but wouldn't take the vows at the final ceremony. Then she would be free to go with Antonio when he came back for her. "I will wait for you, Antonio," María whispered to herself.

Sounds of dishes clanging inside the house startled María. *Olga* . . . María yawned and stretched as she stood up. She realized she hadn't slept all night and suddenly felt exhausted. Even though she spent the night thinking about her situation, she knew her plan was the best solution. *Everything will work out. I know it.*

Chapter 7

Several weeks went by, and summer was soon coming to an end. There was only a week left until Olga would move to the city for nursing school. As it got closer to September, Olga became more enthusiastic about life. She was finally going after her dream to become a nurse. Olga placed an order with Sol y Luna for a few nursing uniforms to look different from ones that were given at the school. She was excited about her new life and wanted to look sharp when she made new friends and hopefully find a husband.

Olga went to Sol y Luna for her final fitting for her uniforms. She made several visits to the shop over the weeks, mostly because she enjoyed her talks with Señora Medina.

"Imagine if a doctor becomes interested in you," Señora Medina said. "How amazing would that be?"

Just the thought of marrying a doctor gave Olga butterflies. "It would be a dream come true," Olga said as Señora Medina put the final pins on the hem of the uniform. "I can't wait to get to the city and start my new life. Of course, I will miss Abuela and my sisters, but my heart has always been with nursing. I have waited a long time for this."

Señora Medina smiled at her. "You deserve it, Olga. You have spent the past many years helping your grandmother with the girls and neglected yourself. This is the time to take care of Olga. Enjoy it, Mami."

With tears in her eyes, Olga hugged Señora Medina tight. Although she was only ten years older than her, Señora Medina always spoke to her in a loving way, as a mother would. Olga would miss her the most.

Olga went into the dressing room to change out of the uniform. "I can have the uniforms ready for you to pick up by Friday," Señora Medina shouted from the other side of the curtain.

Olga stepped out from the dressing room with a big smile on her face. "Perfect, I can't wait!"

"I've never seen you so happy, Olga," Señora Medina chuckled. "Make sure you don't let anyone steal your joy."

"I won't, Señora. I intend on holding onto this feeling for a long time," Olga winked.

As Olga gathered her belongings to leave the store, Señora Medina changed the topic of conversation. "How is María? It's been two days; is she still sick?"

Olga rolled her eyes and responded. "You know María. If she sneezes, she thinks she has to go to the hospital. She's fine. I think she ate some food from Chacho's food stand, and she's paying for it. Abuela told her many times not to eat from there, but you know how stubborn María can be."

They both started laughing. María was probably the most stubborn person they had ever met, but they knew she had a good heart for people.

"Well, tell her that we miss her. If she can't come into work tomorrow, I understand," Señora Medina said, walking Olga to the door.

"I will let her know," Olga promised. "See you Friday!" Olga started her walk home, smiling from ear to ear. The opportunity that she was given had been a blessing. Everything was falling into place, and the timing was just right. Had she gone to nursing school straight out of secondary school, Abuela would not have been able to handle María and Magdalena alone. Now with María going to Altagracia and Magdalena preparing for secondary school, Abuela didn't need her. "Thank you, God," Olga whispered to herself.

Olga made it home quickly to help Abuela with baking. To earn money for the house, Abuela made birthday and wedding cakes. This weekend, Abuela had an order for two wedding cakes and needed Olga's help to decorate. Abuela worked in a bakery for years until her daughter died. She retired from the bakery to stay home and raise the girls. Instead of selling her daughter's house to the government, Abuela decided to rent the home to have monthly income to care for granddaughters. She planned to gift the house to the first to get married, which should be Olga since she was the oldest. However, Abuela had to hold on the house a little longer since her eldest granddaughter had yet to find a suitor. The city will be good for her in many ways.

Olga was putting the pink floral designs on the top layer of the cake with precision. Every time she helped Abuela with the wedding cakes, it gave her hope that one day she would have a cake of her own. Since Olga was a little girl, she planned for that special day: the dress, theme colors, flowers, and cake. All she needed was to be asked that fateful question.

"Señora Medina asked for María again," Olga said as she finished the last flower. "She wanted to know if María was going to be at the shop tomorrow."

"I'm not sure," Abuela answered with her hands on her hips, taking a break from the baking. "I called for Dr. Negron to stop by and take a look at her. She may have mild food poisoning, but I want to be sure it's not worse, like the flu."

Olga shook her head. She couldn't believe Abuela was going so far as to calling the doctor. María was always making things bigger than they were. Her reality was always a little on the dramatic side. Altagracia would fix that in no time.

Just then, María walked into the kitchen in search of food. "Well, hello, Princesa. Nice of you to join us," Olga teased.

"Very funny, Olga," María said, rolling her eyes.

"How are you feeling, nena?" Abuela asked, feeling María's forehead.

"I'm better. I'm just hungry," María said, rubbing her stomach.

"You've been working a lot of hours the last few weeks and eating at Chacho's. There's nothing wrong with you but fatigue and bad pinchos," Olga chuckled. Abuela gave Olga a look indicating that she'd be wise to stop teasing her sister.

"I made some soup," Abuela said, pointing toward the stove. "Eat some before the doctor gets here." María grabbed a bowl ready to savor Abuela's infamous chicken soup. The hearty dish reminded her of her mother since it was her favorite. Packed with carrots, yuca, plantains, and chicken, Abuela's soup was the ulti-mate in comfort food. However, María served herself a bowl of only broth.

"Why aren't you eating any of the vegetables," Abuela asked, slightly offended.

"I want to start out slow. I'll eat more later," María replied. As María slowly drank her soup, the ladies finished the second cake and packed it up in the boxes. Abuela looked at her watch. She finished the cakes thirty minutes before the scheduled pick-up time.

"Gracias a Dios," Abuela said with excitement, as she did the sign of the cross and kissed her thumb. She always gave thanks to God when she completed a cake order. A heavy knock on the front door startled everyone.

"Looks like they're early," Olga said as she walked toward the front door. "We finished right on time." Abuela washed her hands and took off her apron to quickly make herself presentable for her clients.

Olga returned to the kitchen with a smirk on her face. "It's Dr. Negron. He's waiting in the sitting room."

Abuela almost forgot that she called for him. María started to get up from the table when Abuela noticed she didn't finish her soup. "María, you barely ate anything."

"I'm sorry, Abuela. My stomach was not ready for food."

Abuela raised an eyebrow, skeptical of María's response. She was happy that the doctor was there to get to the bottom of this.

"Dr. Negron," Abuela said as she walked into the room. "Thank you so much for stopping by on a Saturday. I didn't want María to wait until Monday to go to your office, and the clinic is so crowded on the weekends."

"First of all," the doctor responded as he hugged Abuela, "What's with the formalities? Call me Tito. You are like family to me. And you can call me anytime." Dr. Negron had an endearing smile on his face when he looked at Abuela. "Girls, did you know that your grandmother used to tutor me when I was in primary school?"

"We know," Olga said with her arms crossed." You tell us that story every time." They all started laughing because it was true.

"Well then, let's check out our little patient here," Dr. Negron said, signaling María to lie down on the couch. Olga went to her room, not interested in the pointless examination. Dr. Negron started with the usual, blood pressure, eyes, ears, and throat check. He poked around María's abdomen and listened to her heartbeat, all the while not saying a word. He only hummed a silly tune that started to annoy María.

"Señora Garcia," he paused from the examination, "would you happen to have some of your delicious limeade?" Abuela instantly blushed.

"Oh, Tito. You remember my limeade?"

"Of course, I do," the doctor exclaimed.

"Let me go pick some limes from the tree in the back and make some for you," Abuela said with a jolt of excitement. Dr. Negron watched as Abuela left the room and listened until she closed the back door.

"María, when was your last period?" he quickly asked.

"I don't know," María responded, perplexed by the question. "I don't pay attention to that."

"María, I'm going to ask you a question, and I need you to be honest with me," Dr. Negron said in a low voice.

"Of course," María said, suddenly aware of where the doctor was headed.

"Have you had sexual intercourse?" María's eyes instantly filled with tears as she nodded yes. The doctor quickly reached into his bag and pulled out a urine test cup. "María, I believe I know why you've been feeling sick, and I'm sorry, but I have to tell your grandmother."

María's eyes widened in horror. "No, please," María begged.

"María, you are a child. It is my responsibility to tell her," Dr. Negron spoke in a tender voice. The thought of having to break the news to Abuela pained him. "I need you to go to the bathroom and pee in this cup so I can take it to the lab for confirmation."

María started shaking uncontrollably and could barely hold the cup. "Please, Dr. Negron. You don't understand," María pleaded.

"I do, María," the doctor replied in a whisper. "I understand."

María got up slowly, suddenly too weak to walk. Her legs felt like noodles as she made her way to the bathroom. She knew the minute Abuela found out, her life was over. The fear of Abuela's wrath was greater than the fear of knowing that she was only fifteen, unmarried, and pregnant.

Dr. Negron paced in the sitting room as sounds of Abuela preparing the limeade in the kitchen filled the air.

"Here we are," Abuela said, holding a tall glass of limeade just as María walked out of the bathroom holding the cup of urine. "What's going on?"

Dr. Negron grabbed the glass and said, "I've missed this so much," with a nervous chuckle. He drank the entire glass full of limeade. "Better than I remembered," he said, still chuckling.

"Tito, why are you taking María's urine?" Abuela asked with her eyebrows raised just as before.

María's eyes were bloodshot from all of the crying, and she avoided eye contact with Abuela. Dr. Negron cleared his throat and motioned Abuela to sit in the chair.

"Señora Garcia, I've examined María, and based on my findings and her response to my questions, it is my conclusion that—" Dr. Negron paused, searching for the right words.

"What is it, Tito? What's wrong with my granddaughter?" Abuela snapped.

"Señora," Dr. Negron straightened up and now spoke in a professional tone. "María is with child."

Abuela immediately stood up. "That's impossible. María is a virgin. She is going to be a nun."

"Señora Garcia, I am going to run a test for confirmation, but I am 99 percent sure I am right."

Abuela turned to look at María standing there, shaking. "María, you've laid with a boy?" Abuela asked in a low voice. María could barely get the word out before Abuela shouted, "Answer me!"

"Olga came running out of the bedroom. "What is going on out here?"

"María," Abuela started again. "Answer my question. Have you laid with a boy?" María lifted her head and looked at her grandmother in the eyes and said yes. Instantly, Abuela lifted her hand and slapped María across her face, something she had never done before.

"Señora Garcia," Dr. Negron said as he held her arm. "Please sit down." He didn't know what to say or how to calm her down.

"Olga, make me some hot tea," Abuela said. Still in shock by what she just heard, Olga ran into the kitchen and pulled out two mugs for tea. She would need some too.

"I'm going to take this to the lab now and send you the results by Monday," the nervous doctor said.

"You don't have to, Tito," Abuela said with her head in her hand. "I had a feeling about María's condition, but I didn't think it was possible. All the signs pointed to this truth. She even missed her cycle, but I didn't want to believe it. You can run the test if you want to, but we already know the results."

"I'm sorry, Señora," Dr. Negron said as he grabbed his medical bag.

Before he made it out the door, Abuela responded, "Gracias, Tito. For everything."

Olga brought the cup of hot tea to her grandmother. "Abuela, your clients are at the back door." Abuela took a quick sip of tea and went to attend to her business.

María sat on the couch, still holding her cheek where the sting from the slap remained.

Olga looked at her with contempt. "What happened to you, María? Just because one boy looks twice at you doesn't mean that you forget who you are and bring disgrace to this family. Did you forget that you were going to the convent while you were messing around with that boy?" Olga laid into her sister hard and behind every word, and there was a hint of jealousy. No boy had ever looked twice at Olga, and here was her little sister, the object of one's desire.

Abuela finished her business with the clients and walked back into the sitting room. Just then, Magdalena returned from her art class at the community center. "Hola familia! Look what I made," Magdalena said, oblivious to the tension in the room. Abuela's gaze was on María, and she didn't notice anyone else in the room.

"María, I cannot put into words how ashamed I am of you. I did not expect this from you," Abuela spoke in a hurt tone.

"What's going on?" Magdalena asked, heart beating fast in anticipation.

"Tomorrow, you will begin a five-day fast. No food and no human interaction. You will stay in the room and away from me while you think about what you've done and pray to God for forgiveness for what you've done to this family. You are no longer the granddaughter I loved. I don't know who you are." Abuela gave María one last look and went straight to her bedroom and closed the door.

"Please, someone, tell me what is going on," Magdalena pleaded.

"You want to know what's going on," Olga snapped. "Your sister is no longer a virgin and is going to have a baby. Our little saint has been with a boy and disgraced the family. Her life will never be the same."

María cried quietly on the couch, thinking the same thing. *My life will never be the same.*

Chapter 8

Three days had passed, and Magdalena was helpless. Several times throughout the day, she would open the door in anticipation of seeing some sign of hope. Each time she was disappointed. Magdalena didn't dare bring it up to Abuela, knowing it was a sore subject. Deep down, she knew it was wrong. Everyone involved was wrong, but Magdalena avoided conflict and usually kept her opinions to herself.

"What are you doing?" Olga whispered in a stern tone.

"Nothing. I . . . I . . ." Magdalena couldn't get her thoughts together.

"If Abuela finds you trying to get in there, you're gonna get it," Olga said, cutting Magdalena off. She gave her sister a stern look, then continued onto the kitchen to help Abuela finish dinner.

Abuela was quiet these days, which was not like her at all. Her face, however, spoke a thousand words. Hurt, anger, and disappointment was all written on Abuela's face. Never would she have imagined her granddaughter would disgrace her family and faith in such a way. Abuela was heartbroken.

Olga placed the last dish on the table and called Magdalena to eat. As they took their seats, Magdalena noticed what Abuela cooked for dinner.

"Pastelón?" she said, shocked. "But that's María's favorite."

"So?" Abuela shouted, with her nose flaring.

"Abuela, I just mean that, she loves pastelón, and she won't be able to eat it," Magdalena explained with her head down, avoiding eye contact.

"It's not my fault she can't have any to eat," Abuela said, still shouting. "There are consequences to each and every action, and María's are just beginning. In two more days, María will be able to eat."

Tears started to well up in Magdalena's eyes. When Dr. Negron told Abuela that María was pregnant, Abuela put María in solitary. She emptied the small room that was used as storage and told María that she had to stay in there for five days. María was to have no food or interaction with anyone. She was to pray and ask God for forgiveness and mercy. Magdalena remembered the look on María's face when Abuela sent her to the room. She didn't say a word or shed a tear. Abuela removed the door knob on the inside so María could not get out on her own.

"María needs to be alone with God and strip herself from everything that will interfere with her pleas for forgiveness," Abuela said when she spoke to her grand-daughters. "No talking to her. No bringing her food. María will stay in the room for five days, and then we will meet with the boy's family."

"Magdalena, eat your food!" Olga snapped, waking her sister from the flashbacks.

They ate in silence, each with a hint of guilt, but fear and pride prevented them from expressing it. After dinner was over, Olga went to her room to continue packing. Olga was beginning her new life in the city, and she couldn't have been happier. Although María was in a tough situation and Abuela had her hands full, Olga couldn't wait to start nursing school. She purchased her bus ticket that morning and was scheduled to leave Saturday after lunch. All she had left to do was get her hair done and pick up her uniforms at Sol y Luna.

Magdalena entered the bedroom, sniffling with watery eyes. Olga watched as she walked to her bed and sat at the edge, looking defeated. "What's wrong with you?" Olga asked insensitively.

"Do you have to ask?" Magdalena replied, wiping her wet cheeks.

"Yes, I do," Olga replied. "Don't let other people's problems become your problem."

"*Other* people?" Magdalena exclaimed. "She's not *other people*, Olga. She's our sister!"

Olga lowered her head in embarrassment. She didn't mean to sound insensitive. She just didn't want Magdalena to slip into a depression over María's poor decisions.

"I'm sorry, Lena," Olga said softly. "Our sister made a huge mistake that will change her life forever. She needs this time to pray."

"Well, I think I need to do the same thing," Magdalena said as she knelt down by her bed.

Olga looked at her sister in sadness. She would miss her, but this situation had shown her that Magdalena would be fine. Witnessing what María was going through was enough to keep her on the straight path. God turns every bad situation good. Her sisters would be just fine.

María splashed water on her face and looked in the mirror. Today was the day; she would finally see Antonio and his family. She hadn't seen Antonio since that night at the beach. He never came looking for her, even after the news of the pregnancy. Surely his mother was to blame. Antonio expressed his love for María so many times before that fateful night; his mother must have stepped in to keep him from seeing her.

Even though María wanted to believe that everything would go well at the meeting, something in the pit of her stomach told her that it wouldn't. She stared at her reflection in silence, waiting to hear that still small voice that she missed. She knew God was angry at her, and she decided to spend the next two years doing penance at the church to earn His forgiveness. If only she had listened to Him before, she wouldn't be in this situation.

Suddenly, María heard a commotion in the other room. Immediately she felt a lump in her throat. It was as if a blanket of fear covered her, and she was paralyzed. A knock on the door from Magdalena confirmed María's suspicions.

"María," Magdalena whispered. "Antonio and his parents are here." Tears started to fill María's eyes. She didn't want to leave the bathroom. "María, are you there?" Magdalena persisted.

"I'm coming," María answered. Taking one last look in the mirror, María called on Mother Mary to intercede on her behalf by quickly reciting a prayer. When María opened the door, she found Magdalena sitting on the floor, waiting for her.

"Oh María," she exclaimed, jumping up from the floor. "Are you ready?"

María simply nodded. She had no choice but to be ready.

Magdalena grabbed María's arm and slowly walked toward the sitting room where everyone was. It was as if María was entering a courtroom to receive her sentence for her crime.

When they reached the room, María took a deep breath and said, "Hello everyone." Her eyes landed on Antonio immediately, but he didn't look at her. His head hung low like someone humbled and guilty. *Oh Antonio, I'm not mad at you . . . Look at me.*

"Sit down, María," Abuela said in an agitated tone. The meeting hadn't officially started yet, and she was already annoyed with the family. It was at that moment that María noticed Olga in the room with Mother Consuela from the convent. Antonio's father was also there and, of course, his mother.

"Magdalena, go to your room," Abuela snapped. Startled, Magdalena quietly headed toward the room, though she didn't close the door so she could hear the conversation in the front room.

"As I was saying before," Señora Morales started talking immediately. "We only came here as a courtesy to you, but we have nothing to do with your situation."

María felt a jolt in her body as if her heart had stopped.

"How can you say you have nothing to do with this?" Abuela quickly responded. "Your son made my granddaughter pregnant."

"So you say," Señora Morales said sarcastically. "There is no proof that my son is the father."

María's eyes widened, shocked by the insinuation.

"My granddaughter was a virgin before she met that boy," Abuela shouted.

María watched how her grandmother passionately defended her character, speaking about the person she no longer was. Pure.

As the two went back and forth arguing about how this came to be, María observed how Antonio didn't raise his head once to look at her, let alone to speak on her behalf. He kept his head low and fiddled with his hands, very much like his father, who never uttered a word. It was clear to her that Antonio took after him.

"Bottom line," Señora Morales continued as she stood up, "Antonio has a big future ahead of him, and I won't let a low-class common girl take that away from him."

"We are not low class, and there is nothing common about my María," Abuela retorted, giving Señora Morales a chilling look. "But you are showing how little class you have by not having the boy own up to his responsibility. They should be married, immediately."

A laughter filled the house that sounded like that of an insane person. Señora Morales dramatically expressed how absurd she thought the idea of the teenagers getting married was.

"Antonio is going to college," Señora Morales said in between chuckles. "He is going to be a lawyer."

María smiled. She remembered when Antonio told her how his mother wanted him to be a lawyer. He wasn't so sure if he wanted the same thing, but his grades were certainly good enough to award him several scholarships. He would make a great lawyer, María thought. He would make a great father too.

Suddenly, Abuela stood up with a shocked look on her face. María was daydreaming again and missed what was said.

"Yes, that's right," Señora Morales continued, with a smug look on her face. "Antonio is going to college in the United States. He will never see María again."

The color in María's face disappeared, and she felt faint. *This can't be happening.* She stared at Antonio, waiting for him to make contact, but his eyes remained fixated on the floor.

"We have nothing else to discuss here," Señora Morales said as she grabbed her purse and headed toward the door with her husband closely behind her.

"Antonio," María said softly. "Why is your mother lying about you leaving the country?" Antonio kept still and didn't respond. "Antonio," María said louder. "Tell me it's not true."

Olga sat with her hand over her mouth, saddened for her sister's pain. Still no word from Antonio.

"Let's go, Antonio," Señora Morales snapped, waiting for her son by the door.

Antonio stood up, eyes red with tears, and whispered to María, «I›m sorry.»

"*I'm sorry?* That›s all you have to say?» María shouted, barely able to catch her breath. "That's all you ever say is, 'I'm sorry.' Was anything you said to me the truth, Antonio?"

Antonio reached for María's hand when Señora Morales shouted from the door, "Now, Antonio!"

Immediately María's hurt expression turned to anger. "I wish I never met you," she said through clenched teeth.

The sting of María's words hurt Antonio to the core. As he turned to walk away, he caught a glance of Magdalena eavesdropping in the hallway with tears running down her face. María wasn't the only one he hurt.

There was a silence that fell on the room after they left. For the first time, Abuela was speechless. María stood in the same spot for a few minutes staring at the door, replaying everything that had happened in her mind. In a manner of minutes, he destroyed her.

"Señora Garcia," Mother Consuela said as she cleared her throat to break the silence. "Abuela," she started.

"Considering the circumstances, María will not be allowed to attend Altagracia. I'm sorry."

"I understand," Abuela replied. "After the baby is born, she can attend next year and continue with the convent, right?"

"I'm sorry," Mother Consuela said, shaking her head. "María is no longer pure. She cannot attend the school or serve in the convent."

"But Mother Consuela," Abuela started but was stopped abruptly.

"It is out of my hands. It is the law."

María continued to stare at the door while the adults talked about her future as if she were not even in the room. Her life was not her own anymore. One moment of weakness changed everything, and none of her plans would work. Abuela and Mother Consuela exchanged a few more words before María noticed the silence. She looked around the room and asked, "Mother Consuela?"

"She left," Olga answered, feeling sorry for her little sister.

Abuela sat in her chair holding her rosary tight. It was hard to determine if she was praying or in deep thought. Her face had an intense look, but she didn't speak a word.

Magdalena found the silence as an opportunity to come out of hiding. She walked right up to María and hugged her tight. That was the first time since the pregnancy announcement that anyone comforted María. Being treated like a leper until now made Magdalena's gesture that more special. María felt her sister's love for her, and the dam broke. María cried and let out all of the tears she fought so hard to keep in. Olga stood up and joined in on the hug. The three sisters held and comforted each other as Abuela watched with a softened heart.

The heartfelt embrace was interrupted by the sound of a car horn outside. After the third honk, it dawned on Olga that it was for her.

"Oh no! I forgot I hired a car to take me to the bus station." Olga ran to gather her suitcase and purse.

"Olga, wait," Abuela said, getting up from the chair.

"Sí, Abuela," Olga said as she fixed her hat on her head, ready to travel to the city. Abuela quickly ran outside to talk to the driver. She looked at her little sisters with a smile. "While Abuela is checking out the driver, come say goodbye." She hugged them one last time and said, "Listen to Abuela. Be good and keep praying. Never stop. Things will get better." Olga picked up her bags and headed toward the door just as Abuela walked back in.

"Did he check out?" Olga asked with a wink and chuckle. Abuela slid her hands in the pockets of her house dress and let out a deep sigh.

"I sent him away."

"What?" Olga asked with wide eyes. "Why would you do that? I have to get to the station. My bus leaves in an hour."

"You won't need the bus," Abuela said hesitantly. "You're not going to the city anymore." Abuela paused long enough to see the horror build up in Olga's face. "I need you here with me to take care of your sisters and the coming baby."

"Abuela!" Olga shouted, never before raising her voice to her grandmother.

"I'm sorry, Olga. You won't be going to nursing school. My decision is final."

"You can't do this," Olga continued to shout as Abuela walked away to her room and shut the door. "You can't punish me for her mistake!" She could barely get the words out as she cried violently.

"Hermana, I'm sorry," María said softly, stunned by Abuela's last-minute decision. Olga's dreams were coming to an end, and it as all her fault.

"Shut up," Olga retorted. "Don't talk to me, you selfish child. I will never forgive you for this." Olga ran into the room and slammed the door. Devastated by the turn of events, Magdalena ran after Olga to console her, leaving María alone.

"What have I done?" María whispered to herself. "What have I done?"

PART TWO
Five Years Later

Chapter 9

María stood in the full-length mirror, looking at how the suit she made fit her. Over the years, her sewing had gotten better, and she was making more women's clothes. Pleased with the fit, María put her hat on and grabbed her luggage. Her new adventure was about to begin.

After the meeting with the Morales family about the pregnancy years ago, Abuela put some rules into place. Olga was forced to stay home instead of going to the city to attend nursing school. Abuela needed her help with the girls and the coming baby. Abuela confined María to the storage room for the duration of her pregnancy. Arrangements were made with the public school for her to do assignments at home with a private tutor. It was challenging, but María was able to keep up with her studies.

María kept her job at Sol y Luna, but she would work from home. Señora Medina would bring her special projects to complete, and María would work on them in the room. In between projects, María would sew baby clothes for a girl and boy. By the time the baby was born, there were plenty of outfits.

Abuela's goal was that no one see María pregnant. María never left the house during the pregnancy. Father Juan came to the house early on to perform the sacrament of confession with María. After that, nuns would periodically visit to pray with María. Sister Rebeca, María's favorite, was the first to visit.

"I miss seeing your face at the church. How are you?"

"I'm not feeling sick anymore," María responded, with her head down, ashamed to look at the nun in the eyes.

"That's good to hear," Sister Rebeca said. "But I want to know about your heart. How are you, María?"

María lifted her head to look at Sister Rebeca. As tears welled up in her eyes, she responded, «I›ve been in this room for four months. No one has ever asked me that question. It's like I don't exist anymore. Only my sin does." María's voice was shaky as she fought back the tears. "The consequences of my actions have affected so many people. Olga doesn't speak to me. Abuela treats me like I'm a stranger. Lena cries every time she is around me. I have never felt so alone in a house full of people."

Sister Rebeca took María's hands in hers and looked María in the eyes lovingly. "You are not alone. The Lord your God is with you. Be strong and courageous, my dear."

"I don't think God loves me anymore. I feel far away from Him," María confessed.

"Have you done the novena?" Sister Rebeca asked. María shook her head no. "I had a feeling you didn't, and I brought a booklet for you. Say these prayers every day for nine days in a row, and God will give you grace."

María accepted the gift of hope in the booklet. She began reciting the prayers that night and for the next nine consecutive nights. On the tenth day, María woke up with the same heaviness she felt the weeks before. She felt hopeless.

The only other person that came to visit María was Ramón. The first time Ramón came to bring fabric and a work order, María was six months pregnant. Ramón stared at María as if he were looking at his own daughter.

"I know I've disappointed you," María said. "I've disappointed myself."

"Mi hija, I only wanted the best for you. And I still do," Ramón hugged María with tears in his eyes, but María barely returned the hug and showed no emotion.

"I remember when we used to talk at the shop about your dreams and—" María cut Ramón off and retorted.

"I'm not that girl anymore."

"María, God forgives you for your sin. You have to do the same," Ramón said as he touched María's cheek. "Peace be with you, mi hija."

By the time María reached full term, her heart had completely hardened. She was distant from her family and the outside world. The only things that kept her company were her thoughts. **You are an embarrassment. You will be a bad mother. God has forgotten you.** Every day she entertained the thoughts, the more she believed them to be true, and the more bitterness planted roots in her heart.

The night María went into labor, Abuela called the midwife and her assistant to help deliver the baby. The two ladies were in the hall talking, not aware that María could hear everything in the bedroom. "Everyone knew the Garcia girls had great futures ahead of them. Well, let's pray that there is still hope for the other two."

María hated having them there during the delivery so much that she gave it her all, and within five hours, María gave birth to a baby boy, Rafael, named after her father.

As soon as the baby was born, Abuela and Olga stepped in. María only got close to the baby to nurse, and even that was hard for her to do. It was hard for her to bond with Rafael as a mother should with her child. María continued to spend time alone in the room either working on school work or clothes for Sol y Luna. Even though the money she was saving for tuition at Altagracia was used to provide for Rafael, she continued to work so she never had to ask Abuela for anything.

By the time Rafael had his first birthday, María finished secondary school. María was diligent with her studies and was able to graduate with her class on time. She never returned to school. The entire time she studied from home. After graduation, she decided to return to the outside world and begin working at the shop again instead of the storage room at home.

María's life was simply going to work and coming home to take care of Rafael. There was nothing else in between. She continued that routine for several years. María had no desire to have a social life, nor did she feel she deserved one.

One day, Señora Medina asked María to meet her at the coffee shop near Sol y Luna. María occasionally would meet her there when she wanted to buy coffee and pastries for everyone at the shop. María would help her carry everything back to the shop. When María walked into Café Con Leche, Señora Medina was sitting at a table near the window, sipping an espresso.

"María, over here," Señora Medina said, waving María over. "Have a seat."

"Aren't we getting coffee for the ladies?" María asked.

"Sit down, María. I wanted to talk to you outside of the shop." María slowly sat down with a confused look.

What could be so important that Señora Medina had to talk to her in private?

"Señora Medina," María said in a trembling voice. "Are you firing me?"

Señora Medina laughed as she grabbed María's hands. "No, sweetheart. I am not firing you. But I am letting you go."

"What," María exclaimed, pulling her hands away from her mentor. "I don't understand."

"María, listen to me." Señora Medina began to explain how much María meant to her, personally and professionally. She has mentored María and watched her grow into an exceptional seamstress. María was better than some of the ladies who had over twenty years' experience.

"María," Señora Medina continued, "I can't keep you forever. It wouldn't be fair to you."

María stared at Señora Medina, still terrified by what she was hearing. None of it was making sense to her.

"I have an old friend from la universidad who has a shop similar to Sol y Luna but bigger. She is looking for a head seamstress, and I recommended you for the job."

"Señora Medina, I love working for you. I don't want to leave you," María said wide-eyed.

"This is a great opportunity for you. She can pay you more and provide you with a studio apartment.

"Apartment?" María asked, confused. "Why would I need an apartment? Is this job in the city?" María asked, somewhat excited.

"Yes and no. It is in the city, but the city is in the United States. It is in Miami." From the moment María heard United States, she was all in. The opportunity suddenly seemed more attractive. It took several meetings with Abuela, but Señora Medina was able to convince her that this was for the best for María. Abuela agreed under one condition: Rafael had to stay with Abuela.

"You need time to get familiar with the job and prepare a good home for Rafael," Abuela said. "Once you find a husband, then you can come back for him."

Of course, Olga was not happy with the plan. She had to help Abuela with Rafael while María went off to her new adventure. She couldn't help but feel bitterness for being put in this situation again.

María was excited to be leaving the town where it seemed everyone knew her. Señora Medina assured María that her past was confidential and her new boss knew nothing. The fresh start was a blessing to María, one she didn't think she deserved. Now at twenty years old, this was just what she needed for herself and her son.

Suitcases in hand, María took one last look at her room and walked out to the sitting room where everyone waited to say goodbye. Señora Medina would accompany her on the trip to help her settle into her new life. This gave Abuela added peace.

"I'm going to miss you, Hermana," Magdalena said, hugging her big sister tight.

"Make sure you write me often," María said. "I want to hear about your college life." Olga stood with her arms crossed as María approached her.

"Hermana," María started, "Thank you for everything. I owe you so much."

"Yes, you do," Olga said sarcastically. "And don't forget it." María smiled, not bothered by Olga's attitude. She went on to embrace her grandmother, but no words were exchanged. Things were never the same between them since the pregnancy. Rafael waited by the door. At four years old, he was very perceptive.

"Mami, hurry up and come back to pick me up, ok?"

María held her precious boy in her arms, and for the first time, her heart was full of love for him. As much as she fought it, she couldn't help but cry as she said goodbye to Rafael. He looked so much like his father. He was a daily reminder of the hurt and betrayal. Today all she saw was a little boy, her little boy, and she loved him very much.

Señora Medina interrupted, "María, we have to go so we don't miss our flight. Ramón went outside to put the bags in the car." Reluctantly, María let go of Rafael and wiped the tears from her eyes. She stood up and took a look around.

"Goodbye everyone," she said, then walked out, closing the door behind her.

"Are you ok?" Señora Medina asked as she handed another suitcase to Ramón to load in the car.

"I will be," María responded with a deep sigh. Ramón closed the trunk and walked over to María.

"Before we go, I'm going to say what everyone else was afraid to say to you. The United States is a very large country. Don't make this move if you think you're going to find that boy and pick up where you left off."

"Ramón," María snapped. "I'm not thinking about Antonio Morales. This is not about him. This is about me and my son and making a better life for us."

"Ok, mija. Then you go and have a blessed life." Ramón kissed María on the cheek.

"Aye ya yaye," Señora Medina yelled. "Can we get to the airport already?" They all laughed as they rushed into the car. María looked out the car window at the house. As Ramón drove away, a feeling of relief came over her. She felt free for the first time in five years.

"Yes," she whispered to herself. "I will be just fine."

Chapter 10

María arrived at the beach just as the sun was going down. Miami Beach wasn't as beautiful as home, but the scenery was still breathtaking. María took her shoes off and allowed her toes to sink in the sand. The cool tropical breeze blew in her hair, forcing María to periodically tuck her hair behind her ears. At the moment when the ocean welcomed the sun, María felt a chill. Hugging herself in an effort to keep warm, María started to rub her bare arms. Suddenly, a blanket was on her shoulders, startling María. Quickly, María turned around only to find Antonio standing behind her.

"You looked cold," Antonio said softly. María blinked hard, not believing it was Antonio looking lovingly in her eyes.

"How . . . what . . . how," María stuttered, unable to get a sentence out. Antonio drew her close for an embrace. María inhaled deeply, taking in the distinct scent of his cologne. It felt good to be in his arms again as if she never left.

"María," Antonio began, "I am sorry for all of the pain I've caused you. I love you very much, and I don't want to be apart from you ever again."

María pulled away to see his face. She opened her mouth to respond, but it was almost as if her tongue had been cut out of her mouth. Frustrated, María tried to formulate the words to respond to Antonio's declaration of love, but she couldn't speak.

"What are you trying to say, María?" Antonio asked. María continued to struggle. "María, what is it? What are you saying?" Suddenly his strong deep voice started to sound like feminine with a heavy accent. A confused María continued with the slurred speech until she woke up to Señora Medina shaking her, saying, "María, what are you saying? You're dreaming, niña."

Confused by her surroundings, it took María a few seconds to realize that she was on an airplane and had fallen asleep. Just then, the pilot made the announcement that they were making their final descent into Miami International Airport.

"We're here, María," Señora Medina said, barely able to contain her excitement.

María was still trying to make sense of her dream that it didn't resonate that she was in another country. The dream marked the first time in years that she thought of her son's father. It was so real it terrified her.

By the time María and Señora Medina went through customs and retrieved their luggage, they were exhausted. The entire traveling experience had been new to María, and although she was tired, she was grateful for the experience.

"Where is Eva?" Señora Medina asked as she scanned the airport for her friend. "I can't find her anywhere."

María didn't bother looking around, considering she knew no one in Miami.

"I'm going to call the boutique to make sure she remembered to pick us up," Señora Medina said as she searched for her phone book in her handbag. "Wait here and watch our luggage while I go use the pay phone."

María was impressed at how comfortable Señora Medina was in the US. She even had a small purse with some American coins in it. Her mentor maneuvered around like Miami was her hometown.

It didn't take long for anxiety to come over María when she realized she was left alone in the middle of all the strangers. As she looked at her surroundings, her eyes met a man standing by the baggage claim area who was looking her way. He smiled at her, and she quickly turned away. "Jesus, Mary, Joseph . . ." María whispered under her breath. She had heard stories about American men and their boldness with women. Some of them even kidnapped them and turned them into prostitution. Realizing that she stood out like a sore thumb, María pulled the luggage closer to her and kept her head low.

Eventually, her curiosity forced her to slowly turn around to see if the man was still looking at her. When she didn't see him by the baggage claim area, María exhaled in relief.

"Hello," a calm voice said that made María jump. It was the strange man, now two feet away from her.

"My . . . my friend is coming back," María said, nervously stumbling over her words and holding her handbag under her arm.

"Ok," the man said, looking intently at María.

"Please don't take me," María begged as her voice shook in fear. The man looked at her bewildered and reached to touch María's arm.

"No!" María screamed and stepped back, stumbling over the luggage. Just then, Señora Medina walked back from the pay phones.

"Carlito, is that you?" Señora Medina shouted as she hurriedly walked toward the man, greeting him with a kiss and a hug. "I just called the boutique, and Eva said she sent you to pick us up." Señora Medina glanced over at María, whose face was beet red from embarrassment. "How did you find María?" she asked.

"She is exactly how you described," the man said in the same soothing voice. "Allow me to introduce myself. My name is Carlos Alvarez."

María's hand met his and shook it slightly, avoiding eye contact. "Nice to meet you," she whispered.

"Trust me, the pleasure has been all mine," Carlos responded with a chuckle. Just as María was about to apologize for her misunderstanding, Carlos picked up the bags and started to walk toward the exit. "Ladies, my car is right out front." Señora Medina and María followed him outside where there was an overwhelming amount of cars and buses picking up travelers. When María saw the blue Pontiac that Carlos walked to, her heart nearly stopped.

"Are you ok, niña?" Señora Medina whispered. "You look pale."

María simply nodded that she was fine. How could she tell her that Carlos was driving the exact same car that Antonio drove back home? The same car that the both of them escaped in that unforgettable night.

The thirty-minute drive from the airport to the boutique seemed like an eternity. Señora Medina and

Carlos talked the entire time as if María wasn't there. They drove up to a two-story building. The first floor was split between two businesses: Eva's Fashions and Valerio Accounting.

A slender woman stood outside wearing white slimming pants with a yellow loose-fitting halter top. Her head full of loose caramel curls fell slightly below her ears. She quickly took one last drag of her cigarette and flicked it on the floor and stepped on it with her white ballet flats.

"Bienvenida," the woman said as she dashed to the car. Señora Medina jumped out of the car and embraced her longtime friend.

"Eva! Look at you," she said excitedly. "You look amazing."

María agreed. The woman was stunning. She leaned against the car and watched the two ladies take turns complimenting each other. María took a deep breath and looked at her surroundings, still trying to grasp the fact that she was in another country. For a moment, she thought about her sisters. They would have enjoyed the flight. Magdalena would have been intrigued by the stewardesses who attended to everyone on the plane. Olga would have complained the entire flight but still enjoyed it.

"Are you daydreaming?" Carlos asked as he took the luggage out of the trunk.

"No . . . not really," María replied, lowering her head, still embarrassed from earlier.

"Well, you're in Estados Unidos now," Carlos continued. "This is the place where dreams come true." María looked up and locked eyes with Carlos. He smiled at her and winked, causing María to blush.

"María," Señora Medina called out. "Come over here and meet Eva."

María hurried over where the ladies were standing. "Eva, this is the girl—woman I was telling you about," Señora Medina started. "She has been my protégé for many years, and now I hand her over to you." Eva had her arms folded, and she inspected every inch of María.

"First of all," Eva began, "we have to do something about your clothes. If you are going to work for me, you have to look fashionable."

"Si, Señora Alvarez," María responded.

"Second of all, we don't have to be so formal. Call me Eva."

María smiled and nodded her head in agreement.

"And lastly, welcome home. I'm sure you are going to love it here." Eva unfolded her arms and extended them toward María for a hug. María felt less intimidated now that Eva welcomed her to Miami and her business.

"Carlito, show María to her accommodations," Eva instructed.

María followed Carlos to the side of the building where Valerio Accounting was. There was a separate entrance that led to the second floor apartment. When Carlos opened the door to the apartment, he yelled, "Ta-da!"

María laughed nervously and walked into the quaint apartment. "This is your new home," Carlos said with his hands out as if he were presenting a grand prize.

María had never been in such contemporary accommodations. She had only heard of the apartments in the city, but she couldn't imagine that they were anything like this.

"Let me give you a tour," Carlos said as he pointed out the living room, kitchen, bathroom, and bedroom.

"This is where I sleep," María asked staring into the bedroom.

"Well, that's what people do in bedrooms, among other things," Carlos joked.

"No, I meant, I've always had to share a room with my two sisters. I've never had a room all to myself." María wasn't counting the eight months she spent in solitude in her grandmother's storage room.

Carlos brought the rest of María's luggage in and handed her the keys.

"If you need anything, just let me know." María nodded her head. "After all," Carlos continued, "I'm only a few steps away."

"Excuse me?" María asked, confused.

"My office is downstairs. I own Valerio Accounting. It is tax season now, so I am in the office until 10 pm most nights."

Impressed by his business owner status, María's eyes opened wide and said, "That's amazing. You are so young to own your own business."

Carlos smiled and looked down in humility. "God has been good to me." The sweet silence in the room was interrupted by the sound of footsteps coming up the stairs. María could hear Eva and Señora Medina's voices getting louder and then the knock on the door. She quickly looked at Carlos.

"Go ahead," Carlos said as he put his hands in his pockets. "This is *your* apartment."

The sound of that made María feel empowered. She dashed to the door and opened it to welcome her guests.

"Aye, María," Señora Medina exclaimed. "Look at your little place, niña."

María couldn't stop smiling from all the excitement that finally caught up with her. The ladies sat down on the kitchen table to discuss the new job. As Eva explained the basics of the job, María noticed Carlos sneak out the front door. Just as he thought he made it without getting caught, his eyes locked with María's. He gave her a wink and a smile and closed the door.

"So for the next two months," Eva continued, "you will work Monday through Saturday. After the communion and prom rush is over, you will go down to a normal schedule." María didn't mind the hard work. She was confident that she would enjoy working and learning from her new boss.

Hours had passed before the ladies left. Eva had picked up a pizza from the corner pizzeria so María could experience an American meal. After they ate dinner, Señora Medina left with Eva since she was staying at her house. As she cleaned up, she thought about her new life and the life she left behind. *Rafael . . .*

That night before she went to bed, María took out a pen and sheet of paper from her travel bag. At the top of the paper, she wrote, *Dear Abuela.* María paused for a moment, suddenly unsure of what to write. Ever since her pregnancy, the relationship with her grandmother had been strained. She closed her eyes and took a deep breath. Putting pen to paper, María continued her letter.

How are you? I made it safely to Estados Unidos. Miami is not what I imagined, but of course, it's only been one day. How is Rafael? I miss home so much. Once I start to receive payment for my work, I will send provisions for Rafael. Until then, may the Lord bless you all.

María

María carefully folded the letter and placed it in the envelope so Señora Medina could deliver it for her. Suddenly, María was fully aware that she was in an apartment alone. This was her life now. There was no one to rely on but herself. She would make it and prove to her family back home that they were wrong about her future.

María searched her handbag for her rosary. Sister Rebeca gave it to her on one of her visits during María's pregnancy. "Don't forget the church," she emphasized. It wasn't a hard thing to do. María couldn't forget how the church treated her when she needed them most. She couldn't forget the whispers at the colmado or the looks at San Lucas. Sister Rebeca was the only one from the church who didn't turn her back on María. Even after Rafael was born, the church would only baptize him privately on a weekday afternoon when no one was around. María understood that she received what she deserved, but it still hurt, nonetheless.

Holding on tightly to the rosary, María knelt at the foot of her bed and whispered a prayer. "Thank you, Lord, for bringing me safely to Estados Unidos. Please watch over Rafael while I'm away. Take care of Abuela and my sisters. Mother Mary, pray for all of us that God may continue to protect us, even though we—even though *I* am not worthy. Amen."

María crawled into bed and placed the rosary under her pillow. A feeling of heaviness came over her, and as tears streamed down her face, María fell asleep.

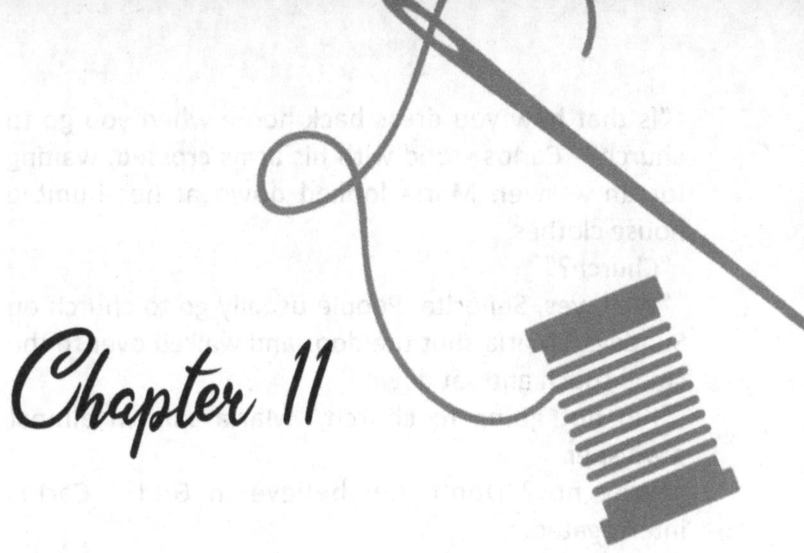

Chapter 11

Sunday morning, María woke up early as she always did. She didn't get much sleep the night before, being in a new country alone in an apartment. Tossing and turning throughout the night, María kept thinking about her new life and the old life she left behind. Rafael was her motivation now. As soon as she had enough money saved, she would send for him.

After preparing a light breakfast for herself, María started cleaning up when a knock at the door startled her. María leaned against the door and asked in a nervous tone, "Who is it?"

"Carlos Alvarez," the voice responded. María quickly straightened out her clothes and fussed with her hair, making sure she was presentable. There was something about Carlos that intrigued her, and her heart fluttered, knowing he was on the other side of the door. María took a deep breath and opened the door.

"Buenos días," María greeted with a smile.

"What are you wearing?" Carlos asked abruptly as he welcomed himself in to the apartment.

"What do you mean?"

"Is that how you dress back home when you go to church?" Carlos stood with his arms crossed, waiting for an answer. María looked down at her humble house clothes.

"Church?"

"Well, yes, Señorita. People usually go to church on Sundays." María shut the door and walked over to the small couch and sat down.

"I'm not going to church," María said in almost a whisper.

"Why not? Don't you believe in God?" Carlos interrogated.

"Of course, I do," María declared, locking eyes with Carlos. "I just don't attend Mass like I used to. I haven't been kind to God, so the church hasn't been kind to me."

Carlos unfolded his arms, suddenly feeling compassion for María. He silently walked over and sat next to her. "I know that sometimes the church can be unkind and cruel," Carlos began, "but God is good all the time, and He forgives."

María smiled and looked down at her hands. "I'm not going to ask what you did, but I know for sure God is waiting for you to come back to church." Carlos put his hands on top of María's and smiled. "I'll wait for you outside."

As soon as Carlos walked out the door, María ran in to the room to change her clothes. She was willing to go to church where no one knew her or her sin. Maybe God would forgive her in America since it seemed as though He didn't back home. Within minutes, they were on the way to Saint Michael's Church. María felt a mixture of emotions, including anxiety, but somehow being with Carlos made her feel like it would be just fine.

Señora Medina and Eva were already seated inside the church. María walked in, amazed at all the stained glass and statues of saints. The church looked nothing like what she was accustomed to back home. Carlos caught María standing in awe of the architecture and beauty of the church. She watched as the people entered the sanctuary gathering for Mass. Her eyes landed on a group of nuns sitting near the front of the altar, waiting for the processional.

"María, are you ready to go sit down? They are about to begin," Carlos said.

"Yes, of course." María walked inside and sat in the second to last row.

"Eva and Estella are saving seats for us up front," Carlos whispered, standing over María.

"No, thank you," María replied. "I want to stay back here."

"But there are so many empty pews, and Eva—" Carlos was cut off when an usher urged him to sit down because the processional had started. He quickly sat down next to María.

"Thanks a lot," Carlos whispered agitatedly. María giggled. "It's not funny!"

The Mass started, and they were forced to stay in the back. María held her rosary in her hand throughout the service and participated wholeheartedly. Toward the end of the Mass, it was time to celebrate the sacrament of Holy Communion. Row by row, people went up to the altar to receive the host and wine. When it was time for their row, Carlos stood up and walked into the center aisle, waiting for María to go in front of him.

"No, I'm not going," María whispered as others crossed in front of her to get by. Carlos looked at her for a few seconds, bewildered. He proceeded to walk up to the altar for Communion, perplexed about María all the way. When he came back to the pew, he knelt down to pray. After a few minutes, he sat down and didn't say a word to María. He couldn't understand why she was being shy about her faith.

After the service, Carlos went outside to wait for his sister and Señora Medina. María was trying to catch up to him. She could tell he was annoyed with her, but she couldn't let that bother her.

"Hello, you two," Eva said as she approached Carlos and María outside. "We didn't think you made it." Eva looked a the both of them, aware of some tension.

"Well," she continued, "let's head on to the house. María, you will get to meet the rest of the family today."

"I look forward to it," María smiled.

"Carlito, Estella and I are going to the market to pick up last-minute things. Go on to the house and introduce María to Luz. She will tell her what to do." Carlos motioned for María to walk toward the car. As soon as they started down the street, María broke the silence.

"So, who is Luz?"

"She is my sister's house maid. Since Eva is so busy with the store, she helps her take care of the house and children."

"I don't understand," María said. "How am I going to help her?"

"Today is Pablo's birthday, Eva's husband. She is having a small party for him, family and close friends. Eva will need extra help preparing before all the guests arrive."

María smiled. "It actually sounds fun. Reminds me of back home."

Carlos had a puzzled look on his face, indicating that he didn't see the connection.

"My abuela had a small baking business. She would make cakes and pastries for weddings and communions. When she was getting close to a deadline, my sisters and I would jump in and help her finish. It was a lot of pressure but always a lot of fun."

Carlos watched how María spoke about her family for the first time. He could see how she was fighting back her emotions as her eyes were getting watery.

"It sounds like you miss your family," Carlos commented, eyes back on the road. María turned to look out the car window, hiding her face.

"I've missed them for a long time."

Carlos chuckled and shook his head. "You've only been here barely twenty-four hours."

María didn't respond. In her heart, she knew that the move to America didn't bring separation between her and the family. The disunion happened years ago.

When they arrived at the house, María's excitement suddenly changed to intimidation. Eva's home was bigger than what María expected. Carlos walked in the house like he lived there and blended in with the team of people working on the party details. There were ladies putting up decorations and another set of ladies setting up the buffet tables. A young man played music on the record player with large speakers, and children were running all over the house.

"Senorita, did you hear me?" a woman yelled, tapping María on the shoulder.

"I'm sorry, the music is loud. What did you say?" María shouted.

"My name is Luz. Come with me." María followed the short gray-haired woman to the kitchen where two other ladies were busy creating a feast. "Here, put this on," Luz instructed as she pushed an apron into María's hands. "You will start the fruit salad." Luz handed María a tool that she had never seen before and proceeded to instruct her on how to make perfectly round balls from the watermelon. "I need you to do the entire watermelon and these two cantaloupes, rápido!"

María was fascinated by the task, attempting to make sure every ball was perfect. Focused on the melons, María didn't realize that Eva and Señora Medina had arrived from the market.

"Everything looks wonderful, Señoras," Eva shouted. "I'm going to go change outfits. Guests will be arriving soon."

In a few short minutes, María finished two large bowls of melons and handed it over to one of the ladies to finish the fruit salad.

As guests started to arrive, the house and backyard quickly filled up with people, overwhelming María. There were so many people who attended the "small gathering" that María felt like a lost outsider. Suddenly, a familiar face appeared.

"Hey, where have you been?" Carlos asked, holding a cocktail.

"There are so many people here," María whispered.

"This is nothing. Wait until you see my sister's Christmas party. It goes on for two days!"

"Carlito!" yelled a distinguished-looking man. "You need to tell Jose to play better music. He is boring me with these oldies." The man turned and looked at María and handed her his empty cup. "Get me another rum punch"

"Alejandro, this is María," Carlos snapped. "She is Eva's new seamstress."

"Oh, I'm sorry," Alejandro laughed condescendingly. "The way she is dressed, I thought she was one of Luz's workers."

María stared at the man and returned the empty cup. Without saying a word, she walked away toward the front door.

"Alejandro," Carlos snapped again, pushing his brother away. "Why do you have to be an ass?" Carlos ran after María to console her. He called out her name several times, but María continued to walk swiftly out the door, feeling humiliated. Several guests were on the front lawn talking and didn't notice María storm pass them. Eventually, Carlos caught up to her.

"María, where are you going?"

"I'm going back home," María said through clenched teeth.

"And how do you plan on getting there?" Carlos crossed his arms. María realized she had no idea where she was or how to get home. As she turned to face him, she spoke in surrender.

"Carlos, can you please take me home?" Carlos stepped closer to María so he didn't have to speak as loudly as she was.

"Please don't leave. The party isn't over."

"I don't belong there," María blurted out. "Your friends see me as a maid. I had to put up with people like that back home. I won't deal with that here."

Carlos put his hands in his pocket and sighed. "Alejandro is my brother."

"Of course!" María yelled and started walking down the street again. It was like dealing with Antonio's mother all over again. Carlos reached for María's hand and pulled her to stop.

"Stop being so immature. We're going back to the party. You will have a good time, and I will take you home when I'm ready." María didn't expect Carlos's harsh tone.

"Yes, Mr. Alvarez," she responded sarcastically. Working her hand away from Carlos, she started walking back to the house. María went straight to the backyard to fix a plate of food when Eva was in the middle of giving a toast to her husband."

"You have been a wonderful husband to me and an amazing father to our children. Happy birthday, my love. God bless you with many more." Everyone applauded the loving toast and took a sip of their beverage. María watched how Eva embraced her husband. She looked at him with adoration her eyes. They made a beautiful couple, just like in the novellas.

"One day, you will have a love like that," Señora Medina whispered to María, startling her.

"I don't know about that. I'm pretty sure it will be just me and Rafael," María said, looking down at the floor.

"María, you have to start believing that you deserve good in your life." Señora Medina was always loving toward María, but at this moment, she had a stern tone in her voice. "You have your whole life ahead of you. Don't live it alone."

María smiled at her mentor. She would miss her encouragement.

They finally sat down at the table to eat. Señora Medina introduced her to everyone who walked by, lifting her up and edifying her. After some delicious food, cake, and laughs, María was feeling better about being at the party. She hadn't seen Carlos since their encounter down the street. It had been a couple of hours, and she was worried that he may have left her.

"Let's go inside to cool off," Señora Medina suggested. "It is very hot out here." When they entered the house, there were people dancing in a makeshift dance floor in the living room. A crowd surrounded three couples showing off their dance moves.

As María got closer, she recognized it was Eva and Pablo dancing. They looked great on the dance floor with their bodies in sync. María soon made out the second couple dancing and cringed. Alejandro. He must have been dancing with his wife because they were very close and sensual. The performance was a little too much for María's taste.

There was the third couple that gave María goosebumps. It was beautiful to watch this couple exhibit romance on the dance floor. When the man finally turned around, María locked eyes with him. It was Carlos. *Carlito* . . . A swarm of butterflies fluttered inside María as she felt her face get warm. The last time she had those feeling was years ago when she first met Antonio. María looked away and pretended not to be interested in the display. Her eyes scanned the room to see the faces of the other guests mesmerized by the siblings' performance. They were truly the entertainment of the party.

When the music stopped, a roar of applause filled the two-story house. It was magnificent. Carlos kissed his dance partner on the cheek, showing gratitude for the dance, and walked over to María.

"Let's go." He walked away and started saying his good-byes to his family.

"I will stop by the shop on my way to the airport tomorrow," Señora Medina said as she hugged María tight.

"Be ready to work at 8:00 am, María," Eva instructed. "Tomorrow will be a busy day."

María nodded. "I will be ready. Thank you for inviting me today." As she made her way out the door, María waved goodbye to different people she had met that day, not remembering any names. When she got outside, Carlos was already waiting for her in the car.

The ride back to the apartment was quiet. Carlos had the radio on, and there was a song playing that María had never heard before, yet the lyrics were familiar.

I cannot see you sad because it kills me,
Your little face (full) of sorrow, my sweet love.
It pains me so much, the tears that you spill,
That my heart fills up with anguish.

When the song was over, the man on the radio said it was called *Nuestro Juramento* by Julio Jaramillo. Aware that María was listening, Carlos abruptly turned the radio off as he pulled up to the apartment building. He turned off the ignition and got out of the car and quickly ran to the other side to open the door for María. In silence, he followed her up the stairs to her apartment. When María opened the door, Carlos simply said, "Buenas noches," and walked away. María was dumbfounded as to why he behaved that way. It didn't occur to her that it was a reflection of her behavior earlier.

María prepared for bed, wanting to get a good night's rest before her first day and Eva's Fashions. Rosary in hand, she knelt down beside the bed to pray. As usual, she prayed for Rafael, Abuela, and her sisters. She prayed for the Alvarez family and for their businesses and thanked God for them. "And God, I pray that I am successful at my new job tomorrow and my new start. Amen."

When María laid her head on the pillow, the memory of the dance came to mind. How impressive the Alvarez siblings were in their dance moves. How handsome was Carlos. *Carlito* . . . She caught herself smiling and thinking about him.

"Stop it, María," she said to herself. "Focus on your job and Rafael. Nothing else." María began to recite the repetitive prayers of the Rosary in her head and, within minutes, fell asleep.

Chapter 12

It was prom season in America. The time of year when teenagers in high school got dressed up for the special dance at the end of the school year. Eva's Fashions was very busy with gown orders and alterations. María had never made those types of dresses for special occasions. Señora Medina would always handle those orders personally. María was nervous that Eva was trusting her with the alterations.

"Now María, I've known Estella for many years, and I know how talented she is. She believes in you and your talents. This is why you are here." Eva crossed her arms and took a deep breath. "But I need to see for myself what you can do. Even though you have moved here, your position in my business is not guaranteed." María started to sweat, listening to what her new boss was telling her.

"Yes, of course," María responded, heart racing. Eva opened a garment back and revealed a pink princess ball gown. María's eyes opened wide at the sight of the distinguished gown.

"We have a new client who received this dress from her older cousin who lives in New York. Her cousin is a flat-chested size ten, but our client is a size four but much bigger breasts. Here are her measurements." Eva handed María an order form with all of the information. "I want you to prepare this gown for alterations. Do not cut it. Just pin it and show it to me when you are done."

María's heart felt like it would beat out of her chest as the task at hand made her anxious. Although she had never worked with this type of fabric or style, she was an expert in the details. If there was anything she learned from Señora Medina and Ramón, it was to always pay attention to the details. Keeping a close eye on the clock, María started working on the gown. Her goal was to get the project done before the rest of Eva's staff showed up for work. The last thing María wanted was an audience during this test.

After ninety minutes, María was confident enough to have Eva review her work. Eva looked at the gown on the mannequin at a distance from different angles. Putting the glasses on that hung around her neck by a chain of pearls, Eva stepped closer to inspect the details in the placement of the pins. Several minutes went by before Eva finally took off her glasses and said, "María Guadalupe Garcia, welcome to Eva's Fashions!"

María exhaled and laughed nervously. Her skills as a seamstress was the one positive in her life that no one could tarnish. A new sense of empowerment overcame María, and it was just the confirmation she needed at this point in her life.

Slowly, the staff members trickled in for the 10:00 am opening. Eva's set up was different from Sol y Luna. The boutique was on the first floor with a small section in the back for Eva's office, including a sewing station.

Above the store was the sewing studio with ten stations and dozens of racks. When everyone arrived, Eva introduced María to the all-female team.

"Ladies, I want you to meet María Garcia. She relocated to Miami to take the position of Lead Seamstress." Eva paused to allow the ladies to soak in the news, including María. María was not aware she would have the same role in America that Ramón had back home. "As you know, after Tatiana got married, her husband didn't want her working anymore, and we needed to replace her. So, everyone, welcome María!"

There was a mixture of reactions to Eva's announcement. Most of them smiled and clapped, expressing their welcome. However, a few of them remained stone-faced. After a few minutes, Eva informed the team to continue with their projects while she would train María downstairs in the boutique all week. As she hurried down the stairs, Eva whispered, "Quickly, María, before they start asking questions."

A puzzled look blanketed María's face. *What did I get myself into?* Once they were in the boutique and out of earshot of the ladies upstairs, Eve explained the situation María was now involved in.

"Several of the ladies have been with me for years. Actually, Carmen was here when I opened eight years ago, but none of them can help me manage this business. I need someone not only skilled, but I need someone I can trust." Eva sighed, looking to find the words to explain her thoughts without damaging anyone's character too.

"I love Carmen, but she is a gossiper and likes to bring drama. Honestly, I think she watches too much of those telenovelas. I keep her because she is very good at what she does, and she knows a lot of people. Her connections bring in a lot of referral business." Eva could see the worry lines forming on María's face and stepped closer to her new manager.

"Estella tells me that you keep to yourself and that you are smart and focused when it comes to your work. She also says that you can be trusted. That is what I need."

María continued to listen, not saying a word but showing enough emotion on her face to convince Eva that she was still worried.

"I don't know what situation you left behind back home, but you are here now, a new beginning God has blessed you with. Receive that blessing, María."

María managed a smile while fighting back the tears. If this was a blessing, did she really deserve it? "I won't let you down, Eva."

They both smiled and hugged each other, marking the beginning of a mentoring relationship and possibly a friendship.

That week, María worked long hours beside Eva learning the basics of the business. Eva wanted María to be prepared to operate the shop in her place if ever the need arose. Every night María would go up to her apartment, make a quick dinner, and go to bed.

When Sunday morning arrived, María could barely make it out of bed. Regardless of the aches and fatigue, she got out of bed and got ready for Mass. María grabbed the directions Eva gave her to St. Michaels and prepared herself for the walk to church. As she went down the stairs of the building, she could hear music coming from Valerio Accounting. It was the last week of tax season, and Carlos was working fifteen-plus-hour days. She was shocked that he would be in the office on a Sunday. María did her best to walk by the storefront unnoticed, but Carlos spotted her and waved as he walked toward the front door.

"Where are you headed so early this morning?" Carlos asked when he opened the front door.

"I'm going to church." María hadn't seen Carlos following the party at Eva's home, and he had since grown a beard.

"Mass doesn't start for another two hours," Carlos pointed out with a chuckle.

"I'm walking there," María responded quickly. "Considering this is the first time I'm walking, I don't know how long it will take me."

"I'll take you," Carlos said with a big smile.

María couldn't help but look at him skeptically as if he was up to something. "Why do I feel like this will cost me?"

Carlos burst into a deep laugh. "All I ask for is a cup of café con leche and toast. I never went home last night because I had so much work to do, and now I'm exhausted."

"Oh my goodness," María said as she frantically searched her purse for the keys. "Of course. Come upstairs." Carlos quickly turned off the music and lights in the office and locked the front door. By the time he reached María's apartment, the percolator was on the stove brewing coffee.

Carlos made himself comfortable at the kitchen table with his newspaper. He skimmed through the news whispering comments to himself as María quickly scrambled two eggs to add to the toast. It had been a long time since she cooked for someone. It felt nice to do this small gesture for Carlos. He had been very helpful to María since she arrived to America.

"Here you go," María said, serving the breakfast.

"Wow, what a surprise. My stomach thanks you." They both started laughing. María sat at the table and joined Carlos with a cup of coffee. They fell into a conversation about the United States and the condition of the country back home. Carlos was passionate about politics, and María was intrigued by everything he said. Politics was never a subject she was interested in back home, but hearing Carlos talk about the two counties and how their governments could improve stirred an interest in María to learn more.

"You know so much about politics. Why didn't you become a government official like your brother?"

Carlos took a slow sip of coffee and took his time to respond. "I truly love helping people. My brother is more consumed with having power. I can do more good for the community behind the scenes." Carlos went on to explain how he used his accounting business to help immigrants with their residency and establishing themselves in the United States. María was fascinated by what Carlos said and how he said it.

"Well," Carlos said, looking at his watch, "we have to leave now if I'm going to get you to church on time. María all but forgot about her plans to attend Mass that morning. She could have listened to Carlos talk for hours. It almost reminded her of her talks with Antonio back home. The difference was that Carlos talked about helping people and making life better for his country. Antonio only talked about himself and breaking away from his mother's hold. It's a wonder how María had fallen so hard for Antonio to the point of compromising who she was and what she believed in.

When they arrived at St. Michael's, Carlos decided to join María in the Mass.

"I am not used to going to church at eight o'clock in the morning with all of the senior citizens," Carlos joked. There were only a few dozen people in the church, and Carlos and María were the only ones without silver hair. María was not aware that the first service of the day at St. Michael's was usually for the elderly in the community. They would offer them coffee and muffins after the service in the Bingo hall. Back home, María was always up early attending Mass even earlier, and there was always a mixture of congregants.

After the Mass, Carlos took María home and walked her to her apartment door.

"Carlos, I appreciate you waiting and taking me to church today, even though you were tired."

"It was my pleasure," Carlos said with a faint smile, although his red eyes expressed his fatigue. "I don't mind picking you up every Sunday to take you."

María blushed at his kindness, knowing he couldn't possibly be serious. "You don't have to do that. I am fine on my own." The thought that Carlos would really go out of his way for her embarrassed her and scared her at the same time.

"It is no bother. I have to drive past the building on my way to church anyway. I don't mind doing it." María had a dubious look on her face, not sure if Carlos had any underlying intentions.

"Look," Carlos said, wide-eyed, "if it makes you feel better, you can pay me with a café con leche every Sunday morning." María couldn't help but laugh at the shameless request.

"Agreed. One café con leche for one ride to church," María agreed, extending her hand to seal the deal with a handshake. When Carlos accepted her hand, instead of shaking it, he turned it and kissed the top of her hand.

"Agreed," he said, and without another word, he trotted down the stairs and left.

María entered her apartment, not knowing what to make of Carlos Alvarez. Although she was grateful that he offered to take her to church every week, she was paranoid that he had secret intentions to charm her like Antonio did. The more she thought about it, the more it troubled her.

María searched her purse and pulled out the directions to the church that Eva gave her. Determined to prove her independence, she decided to head back to St. Michael's on foot. Walking down the main boulevard, María was able to take in the different businesses in Miami. Since she moved to America, she hadn't had a chance to visit the different tourist attractions. Walking the three and a half miles to St. Michael's was an adventure in itself.

In a little over an hour, María arrived at the church. There was a Mass already in progress. She took the opportunity to sit in her usual spot in the back and rest for a few minutes before walking back home. An uneasy feeling came over her that something wasn't right. As she looked around, she noticed two ladies were watching her on the other side of the church. After a few seconds, María realized that it was Carmen from the boutique, and she smiled and waved. The woman had a look of disgust on her face and leaned in to whisper something in the ear of the other spectator. The two of them continued to openly stare at María, ultimately making her feel uncomfortable. It was a good thing that the Mass was coming to an end and she could escape and head back home.

As soon as the priest made his way out of the church, María exited the pew on her way out also. Carmen quickly did the same and caught up with María outside of the church.

"María," she said with a mouthful of attitude, "don't you think it is disrespectful to show up to church at the end of the service?" María realized how bad it seemed and chuckled.

"Yes, but I actually came to the eight o'clock Mass. I wanted to see how long it would take me to walk here, so I came back."

"Well, how did you get here this morning?" Carmen asked.

"Oh, Carlos brought me."

"Carlito?" The woman with Carmen spoke for the first time. María didn't even notice she was standing there. There was a familiarity about her now that María saw her up close.

"Yes, Carlito," María responded with a smile. "My name is María Garcia. I work with Carmen."

"I know all about you," the woman said with a look of contempt. María was about to ask her what that meant when Alejandro Alvarez interrupted the conversation.

"You left so quickly that I couldn't catch up." María instantly regretted coming back to the church. The sight of Alejandro repulsed her. His arrogance was overwhelming. When he noticed who the ladies were talking to, his face lit up. "Well, hello there. I see you've met my wife." That was it. The woman was at Eva's party dancing provocatively with Alejandro.

"And Vanessa, I see you've met Santa María." María felt the blood leave her face. Why did he call her that? "My sister tells me that you are as good-hearted as a saint,"

Alejandro said, flashing his politician smile as he looked around, wanting to be seen.

"I enjoy what I do and am grateful to Eva for the opportunity."

"I'm sure you are," Carmen interjected, clearly still holding resentment for being passed for the promotion.

"Well, I must be going," María said, anxious to be away from the group.

"Enjoy your walk," Vanessa said condescendingly.

As María walked away, she could hear Alejandro talking. "Of course, she will enjoy the walk. Those kinds of people back home are used to walking everywhere. They can't afford cars." Anger must have fueled María since even in the midday Miami heat, she made it home in less than an hour. María was tired of being looked down on. She thought being in a new environment would be different for her.

"I'm not going to live my life this way." María stared at her reflection in the bathroom mirror. "I will be rich one day, and people will regret that they treated me this way. They will all envy me." A darkness covered María as she let the anger fester within her.

Slowly, the once innocent, warm-hearted María was becoming more hardened. María was gradually building a wall around her and separating herself not only from others but also from God's precepts that were far from memory at this moment. Consumed with a growing anger, she couldn't hear the cries from her spirit.

Do not hasten in your spirit to be angry,
for anger rests in the bosom of fools.

Chapter 13

S ix months had passed since becoming the lead seamstress at Eva's Fashions, and María was finally on a set work schedule with weekends off. Now that Eva announced she was pregnant with her fourth child, due in March, María had to look forward to managing the business alone for a few months after the baby was born. María wasn't nervous about it at all, especially after earning the respect of the ladies at the shop. Even Carmen softened a little, although she was still bitter about being slighted for the promotion.

On the way back from the supermarket, María stopped to pick up the mail at the boutique. On Saturdays, Eva had a part-time sales woman overseeing the store operations. Rosa was a lovely middle-aged widow who came to the United States as a child. She had a flair for fashion, and every outfit she wore complimented her Coke bottle figure. Rosa worked at Eva's Fashions simply because she loved it. She lost her husband in a tragic factory accident years ago before having the chance to have children. A large settlement was awarded by the manufacturer that would last Rosa a lifetime. Between her charity work and her painting, Rosa kept busy and content.

"Buenos días, Rosa." María walked through the door, hugging two paper bags full of groceries.

"Hello darling. I have your mail for you right here." Rosa grabbed the small pile of catalogs and envelopes from behind the counter and placed them in one of the grocery bags.

"You read my mind," María said, still holding on to the two bags. "Have a great rest of the day." María was an expert now with going up the stairs with her hands full. Within minutes, she had all the groceries put away and was relaxed on the couch sorting through the mail. Eva subscribed her to several trade magazines and store catalogs so she could keep current with the fashion trends. María loved spending a quiet afternoon going through them while soft music played in the background.

As María skimmed through the envelopes, the handwriting on one of them made her heart skip a beat. *Abuela.* María had sent six letters and at least four money transfers to her grandmother since she moved. This was the first response she had received from her grandmother. María sat up straight and stared at the envelope in her hand, afraid to open it. Suddenly she was the teenager again, the one who brought shame to her family. Why did it take Abuela so long to write? Was the humiliation of María's disgrace still upon the family back home?

After what seemed like an eternity, María cautiously opened the envelope and removed the delicate stationary. Taking a deep breath, she unfolded the sheets revealing the message from her grandmother.

Dear María,

I received your letters over these past few months. I'm sorry that I haven't responded, but it has been hard accepting the direction your life has taken. I would have never imagined that you would be living in another country, unmarried, and with a child who doesn't even live with you. I know I gave my blessing for you to leave, but that doesn't mean I like how things have turned out.

We received the money you have been sending for Rafael also. Do not worry, he is being treated like a prince. He asks about you every day. He wants to know if you have found his father yet because he is ready to be with you in America. I don't know where he got the idea that you left to look for his father. I pray to the good Lord that you did not do that. I pray that you are smarter today than you were when you were at fifteen.

Olga has been doing a great job taking care of him. While he is in school, she helps me with baking. It's been busy lately with so many weddings and quinceañeras.

Magdalena is attending art school in the city. She received a scholarship to the college and lives in student housing. She has a medical student who has asked me permission to court her. He comes from a good family. I am certain he will marry her. I was worried about her and her free spirit, but I am very proud of her and the young woman she has become.

I will light a candle for you at church and continue to pray for God's mercy on your soul.

With love,
Abuela

Tear drops stained the stationary as María read the letter a second and third time. Abuela's cold tone and selection of words proved that she still hadn't forgiven María for her sin all those years ago. No matter how hard she tried, her grandmother would always see the sin and not the woman.

As she stared at the letter, her sadness began to change into bitterness. María thought about ways to respond to Abuela and what she would say if she were in front of her. Different scenarios of how the conversation would go went through her mind, conversations that would never happen.

Before she knew it, an hour had gone by. María put the letter back in the envelope and placed it in her nightstand drawer. As far as she was concerned, she was not going to read the letter again. If Abuela wanted to treat her as a stranger, then she was more than happy to do the same.

An unexpected knock on the door startled María since she wasn't expecting anyone. She didn't have any friends or family in Miami. The only person who would visit her was Carlos on Sunday mornings. She enjoyed those conversations over breakfast with him before going to church. It had been three weeks since she'd seen him. He had some personal obligations that kept him from making it to Sunday Mass but promised he would be back this week. When María opened the door, Rosa stood there holding a large package.

"The mailman just came back and delivered this package for you. It looked important, so I brought it to you right away." Rosa handed María the package. María studied the package trying to make out the smeared return address. The only legible writing on the package read AIR MAIL. "Were you expecting a package?"

"No, I have no idea what this is," María said as she walked to the kitchen table. Rosa followed her to the kitchen, just as curious. The two ladies sat in silence as María used a knife to open the mysterious box to reveal a large manila envelope. María quickly opened the envelope as the suspense was starting to annoy her. Inside the envelope were three more envelopes. María opened the first one, and it was a card from her grandmother that said Happy Birthday on the front of it.

"María, it's your birthday?" Rosa asked with excitement. María smiled and nodded. She thought Abuela had forgotten about her birthday since she never acknowledged the day after getting pregnant with Rafael.

"My birthday is tomorrow." Fighting the tears, she read the card from Abuela that wished her a happy birthday and blessed her with a good year. "It's from my abuela," María explained to Rosa as she grabbed another envelope. It was a birthday card from her sisters. She had no communication with her sisters since moving also. This was a pleasant surprise reading the well wishes from the girls. As María read the card, Rosa asked her if she could open the third card for her. Without looking up from the card, María nodded yes. Before María realized what she had just agreed to, Rosa let out a screech.

"You have a son?"

All color left María's face as she stared at Rosa, at a loss for words. Rosa stepped closer to María and put her hand on her shoulder. She could sense that María felt uncomfortable.

"María, you have a beautiful little boy?" Rosa handed her the card and inside was a picture of Rafael. María burst into tears at the sight of her son. He had grown so much in just six months. The card simply said, "I miss you, Mami."

Rosa handed María a handkerchief and helped her to the sofa. María's crying continued now because her secret was exposed. "Rosa," she managed between sniffles. "Please don't tell anyone about this." Looking deep into her friend's eyes, she held her hand and enforced her request. "I don't want anyone to know. Please keep my secret."

"Of course, darling. I won't say a word." Rosa squeezed María's hand.

María was grateful that Rosa was the one to find out about Rafael and none of the other lades in the shop. She trusted Rosa and believed she was a woman of her word.

"Can I pray for you, María, dear?" Not knowing how to answer, María shrugged her shoulders. No one had ever asked her that question. "Sweet heavenly Father, I come before you on behalf of my dear friend, María. Lord, I do not know the fullness of her secret, but you do. Father, today I ask that you bring her peace regarding this situation. Lord, dry her tears and comfort her heart. She misses her family dearly. Father, please fill that emptiness with your love and peace that goes beyond understanding. Let her know that you are her refuge and that she is not alone. Bless her, Father. Bless her family back home and bless her precious little boy. All this I ask in your name, sweet Jesus." When Rosa opened her eyes, María's face was wet from an overflow of tears.

"No one has ever prayed for me before. I've never heard a prayer like that."

Rosa embraced her in a nurturing way. "I just spoke from my heart, darling." Rosa pulled away and looked warmly at her friend. "I don't know what you are going through, but I do know that our Father has got you in the palm of His hand. He loves you, darling."

María smiled, grateful for the kind words but certain that not all of it was true. She was sure God had not forgiven her for her sin yet.

"María, have you invited Jesus into your heart? Do you acknowledge that He is your Lord and Savior?"

"Of course, I know that He is my Lord," María retorted, taking offense. "I am Catholic."

"I know, dear. I meant no harm. I know that you go to church every week, and I've seen you with your rosary, but do you have a personal relationship with the Lord?"

The questions made María feel uneasy. Why was Rosa asking her this? Was she judging her too, just like the other church members back home?

"My relationship with the Lord is fine, thank you." María stood up. "If you don't mind, Rosa, I have a lot to do today."

"Yes, I'm sorry," Rosa apologized, standing to her feet. "I actually have to pick up a dear friend from the airport. She is flying in from Texas. She is a widow like me, and she just started her own cosmetics company. I'm so excited to see her." As she hurried out the door, she waved at María. "I'll bring Mary by sometime this week so she can meet all of you. Be blessed, my friend!"

As María shut the door, a tear fell down her cheek. How could a woman encourage her one minute and insult her the next? Slowly she sat back down on the sofa and picked up the cards, taking her time to read each one again. Her heart ached for each member of her family. She was missing her role as big sister to Magdalena just when she needed her most. Her guilt for Olga missing out on nursing school would be with her for the rest of her life. Although she was a pain most of the time, she missed her big sister very much. Things were never the same with her grandmother. Even though the birthday gesture was not consistent with Abuela's behavior the last five years, María was touched deeply. As much as Abuela wanted to, she couldn't write María out of her heart. This was proof she still remained there.

María gathered the picture of Rafael and his card and put it back in the large envelope and took it to her bedroom. The only place she believed was safe was in between the mattress and box spring. No one would find the secret she had been keeping all of this time. One day the truth would eventually come out, one day when she would have saved enough money and moved to another part of the United States with Rafael. For now, Eva and her family and the ladies and Eva's Fashions could never know about her sin and its fruit.

Chapter 14

The windows were decorated with images of trees and Santa Clause, and carols played in every store. Christmastime was here, and María was in Miami, away from the ones she loved. This was the first time she had ever been so far from her family during the holidays. Even when she was in isolation during her pregnancy, she didn't feel as alone as she did now. María had been working more hours at the shop lately since Eva had been taking time out of the shop to prepare for her annual Christmas party. Her attempt to stay busy and not think about her loneliness was a failed plan. María's only free time was on Sundays, where she spent most of it with Carlos.

María finished setting the table for breakfast since Carlos would be arriving any minute. Just like every Sunday, they had breakfast together and great conversation before attending Mass at St. Michael's.

"Would you be upset if we didn't go to church today?" Carlos asked as he took another sip of café con leche. Her eyes shown wide in shock at his question.

"Why wouldn't we go to church? It's Sunday; it's what we do. It is the one hour a week we devote completely to God."

"I want to take you somewhere. I'm sure God will understand." Carlos looked at her with a debonair smile, making María blush. She tried to hide her attraction to him, but at times, when he flashed that smile, she couldn't help her cheeks from reacting.

"Fine, but you have to tell me where we are going," María demanded, crossing her arms.

"It's a surprise." Carlos stood up quickly and grabbed his car keys. "You might want to wear something a little more comfortable," he snickered. María was not one for surprises, but she found herself jumping at the opportunity with Carlos. She quickly changed her clothes and put on comfortable flats. Within minutes, they were on the road.

As always, Carlos rambled on about the latest political news, but María's mind was far away. The last time a man told her to get in the car for a surprise location, she ended up on the beach with Antonio. As long as she lived, she would never be able to remove the details of that night from her memory. María closed her eyes, and she could still smell the ocean and hear the waves crashing. The evening breeze brought a slight chill and made her shiver when she thought of it. She couldn't forget the way Antonio's touch brought a surge through her body. The taste of passion on his lips remained as if it were yesterday. These bittersweet memories would haunt her for the rest of her life.

Carlos talked the entire drive without noticing that María wasn't paying attention. "We're here," he sang. María perked up and looked around at what seemed like the open markets back home.

"Carlos, is this what it looks like?"

"Even better!" Carlos let out a big laugh as he got out of the car. "You will find all the fruits and vegetables from back home right here. You'll even find seasonings and other various items that you can't get in any store in America." He grabbed her hand and pulled her to keep up with him. Carlos walked with determination as if he knew exactly where he was going. As they passed merchant after merchant, María felt as if she was back home. The people, the foods, and crafts, they all represented the comforts of home right here in Miami.

They finally stopped at a booth where the merchant had stacks of fabrics displayed. "Hola," the woman behind the table greeted with a toothless smile.

"These fabrics," María blurted out, "they are exquisite." The woman explained that they were one-of-a-kind materials imported from a town in the Dominican Republic. Apparently, they were inspired by the same fabrics of up-and-coming designer, Oscar de la Renta, who was from that town and now living in Europe designing for the elite. María was overwhelmed by the different textiles. Her mind raced as she thought of the different dresses she could make.

"Is there one that stands out to you?" Carlos looked at María and how her face lit up. She was like a child in a toy store, bright-eyed and grinning from ear to ear.

"They're all so beautiful, but this one is my favorite." María held up a candy apple red chiffon fabric. "I love the color and the feel of the fabric. It's like silk.

"It is called chiffon, and it looks even better with lace or with these beads." The merchant pointed to another table with containers filled with different kinds of beads.

"Does Eva know about this place? She would go crazy with these selections," María said.

"Yes, Eva knows about this place," Carlos responded. "She keeps it a secret because she only gets fabric here for her elite orders or for herself."

"I don't blame her," María laughed. She looked at more of the different fabrics and the beads, thinking of different things she could make if she had the money. The fabrics were definitely exquisite, but they were out of her price range. "Are we picking something up for Eva?"

"Well," Carlos started as he cleared his throat. "As you know, Eva has her big party coming up in a couple weeks, and I wanted to know if you would honor me by letting me escort you to the party." Carlos had more to say, but he waited for María to respond.

"I don't understand," María said. "I will be there. Eva invited me."

"I know. But I want to make sure you will be there . . . with me."

María was speechless. Carlos was asking her out on a date, something she never had before. Her time with Antonio was of stolen moments, nothing like an official date. Besides, after Carlos, no other man showed interest in María.

"I like spending time with you María. I want to get to know you more. Will you let me court you?"

María couldn't believe what she was hearing. What was Carlos thinking? Why would he want to be with someone like her when he could be with so many other women more deserving?

"I will not let you say no," Carlos straightened up, becoming more confident in his feelings.

"Ok, I will go with you to the party." Carlos's face lit up as he pulled María in for an embrace. Eventually, she would have to tell him about Rafael, but only if things got serious between them. She was sure that Carlos was just feeling sorry for her and didn't want her to be alone for her first Christmas away from family. He may change his mind come the new year, and she wouldn't have to tell him of her past or her son she had out of wedlock.

Carlos pulled away from María and clapped his hands. "So, the reason why we are here is that I want to buy you the materials you need to make a dress for the party. You mentioned that you had nothing to wear, and you didn't know if you would be able to afford a dress at the department store."

"You remember that," María asked, shocked. She told him that weeks ago when she was preparing breakfast one Sunday morning. Carlos was so focused on the newspaper she didn't think he ever listened to her ramblings. A hint of embarrassment arose in her because she couldn't say the same. Carlos rambled about politics all the time, and María listened maybe half of the time.

Suddenly feeling like a princess, María decided to take advantage of the offer and make the dress of her dreams. She had the merchant cut five yards of the red chiffon and two yards of black lace to make a wrap. María always wanted a halter dress like the famous American actress, Marilyn Monroe, wore in an old movie years ago. She had seen the dress in several magazines and wanted to replicate it in red with a black lace wrap to cover her shoulders.

As she talked to the merchant and picked out the materials she needed, Carlos stood, arms crossed, watching María. He wasn't sure what it was that he liked about her. It was true she wasn't like any other girl he dated, but he could see her heart, and it was pure. He liked the way he felt when he was with her. Carlos was ready to settle down, and he could see that happening with María.

Carlos and María ended up spending the rest of the day together, spending most of it at the market and then an early dinner at a local restaurant. The conversation between them was effortless, but María was nervous that the conversation would turn toward her and her past back home. She continuously asked him questions about himself, and the more she learned about Carlos Alvarez, the more she realized how much she liked him.

When Carlos took María home, he helped her up the stairs with the bags of fabric. As they stood at the front door, María suddenly felt nervous. This was different from any other Sunday when he would drop her off after church. He expressed his interest in her, and she didn't hide her attraction to him.

"Thank you for everything, Carlos. I had the best day."

"I like to see you smile. I promise to do my best to make you smile every day," Carlos said with sincerity and tenderness in his voice. María's heart melted. How could this be real? She didn't deserve a man like Carlos. Her life was as stained as the color of the fabric she just purchased. She would just enjoy the moment, and when the time came, she would reveal the truth.

Carlos leaned down and kissed María on the cheek. "Have a good night, beautiful." Every Sunday, Carlos kissed her on the cheek as friends often do; however, his kiss somehow felt different at that moment. María felt her senses go on overload in that split second. From the scent of his cologne when he got close to her to the look in his eyes when he drew back. María was at a loss for words. Carlos headed down the stairs to his car, and it wasn't until María heard the ignition to the car that she un-clocked her door and went inside the apartment.

Almost immediately, María laid out her fabric and started outlining her dress. She planned to work on it a little bit every day during her down time at the shop. Before she knew it, it would be the day of the party, and she wanted to look perfect. All she needed was the right shoes and accessories, and her outfit would be complete. If she could be happy and worry-free for one day, she would do everything possible to make that happen. María was determined to have the best-looking dress, the best-looking date, and have the best time at Eva's party. Even if it was temporary, she was looking forward to a bit of happiness.

Chapter 15

It was the day before the Christmas party, and María was exhausted from working overtime over the past two weeks. The holiday season was very busy for the boutique, and the number of orders for gowns was overwhelming. Nevertheless, there was an adrenaline that fueled María to continue working the long hours. The days leading to the party, Carlos brought meals to the boutique every day, and they ate lunch together. Even in all the busyness, they still found time to spend together, getting to know each other on another level.

Earlier that week, María went shopping for herself for the first time since being in America. Every time she went to a store to shop, it was usually to buy things to send back home. María decided to splurge a little and buy some accessories for the party. Rosa took her to Burdines department store at the Dadeland Mall, where she was able to find everything she needed to complete her outfit.

"You're going to look beautiful for the party," Rosa said as she admired the red pumps María had purchased.

"I hope so. I am nervous about it. I have never been to a formal party, not to mention with a handsome man like Carlos." Just saying his name gave her butterflies in her stomach. María couldn't remember the last time she was so happy. She considered herself lucky to have a man like Carlos Alvarez in her life, even though she knew it wouldn't be forever.

As soon as she had enough money saved, she would send for Rafael. By then, she would have much more experience as a seamstress and knowledge of the United States that she could leave and live in another town where no one knew her. María knew deep down in her heart that the minute Carlos found out about her sin, his feelings for her would change. It was better to protect herself now and plan for what she would do when that day came so it would be no surprise for her.

"María," Rosa started, lowering her voice, "have you told him yet?"

"Sometimes I forget that you know my secret." María walked away to the kitchen to get another cup of coffee. "I haven't told him yet, but I will." It was evident that the topic agitated her.

Rosa could see how María's jaw clenched every time she brought up her friend's situation. "Sweetheart, I don't understand why you continue to keep this from Carlos. He adores you. He will adore your son too."

"You don't know that," María argued. "I have met people like the Alvarez family. They have certain standards, certain people they allow in their circle. Everything may be great now, but as soon as they find out about my reputation back home and what I have waiting for me, they will remove me from that circle immediately."

Rosa could see the hurt in María's face, although she tried to hide it. "Is that what happened to you with Rafael's father?"

"Rosa, I don't want to talk about it. Please."

Letting out a frustrated sigh, Rosa walked up to María and looked her in the eyes. "The more you keep all of this bottled up inside, the more it festers. I am not trying to be nosy here, honey. I am trying to help you." María folded her arms, attempting to thicken the wall she had built up. "You are a beautiful young lady with a wonderful future ahead of you. Don't let bitterness consume you so much that you can't see when God has sent people to help you."

"Stop it," María covered her ears. "Don't say things that aren't true, Rosa. I love you, but you know as well as I do that God is not going to send anyone to help me. I've made my mistake, and for the rest of my life, I will do penance for that." María picked up Rosa's pocketbook from the kitchen table and handed it to her. "Thank you for your help today, Rosa. I will see you at the party."

Stunned by her friend's sudden rudeness, Rosa slowly took the pocketbook away from María and made her way out the door without saying a word.

For a moment, a feeling of regret covered María. Rosa had always been so kind to her, and this was the way she treated her?

María hadn't talked to Rosa since that day in her apartment. The tension at the shop was high. Rosa was her usual cheerful self, helping shoppers and charming them with her Southern hospitality. María had expected her to be sad and upset and burdened by their last encounter. *How could she be so calm as if it never happened*, María thought.

When the day was over, everyone came together to clean up and organize the store. Tomorrow was Sunday, and the shop was normally closed, and Christmas day would be Monday. They wouldn't be back in the shop until Tuesday. María thanked everyone for their hard work and wished them all a blessed Christmas. Not everyone would be at the party, so they exchanged hugs and kisses as they departed. Rosa caught María off-guard and gave her a tight, long hug.

"My dear friend, I only want the best for you. May God bless you and shower you with His love this Christmas!" Tears welled up in María's eyes. After the rudeness, Rosa was still showing her kindness and love.

"Thank you, Rosa. And I'm sorry," María couldn't look Rosa in the eyes, afraid she would see the shame in her eyes.

"Darlin, you've already been forgiven." Rosa squeezed María's hand and looked at her lovingly. "See you tomorrow, dear friend."

The last time María had been to Eva's house was for Pablo's birthday party. The transformation she made to the house with all of the Christmas décor was astounding. For a split second, María felt like she didn't belong there. How did she end up among such extravagance?

Carlos gripped her hand tighter as he whispered in her ear, "You're the most beautiful woman here." A feeling of warmth and fullness came over María. No longer were the feelings of butterflies in her stomach. María now felt peace and comfort with Carlos.

"Thank you, Carlos. I feel beautiful for the first time in years." María was truly happy.

"María?" A voice approached them from behind. María turned around to see her mentor Señora Medina in front of her. "Mi hija, you look amazing! Estados Unidos has been good to you." They held each other in a long embrace.

"I had no idea you would be here," María said, fighting the tears. She owed her new life to Señora Medina. If it weren't for her, María would still be back home living a mundane life. Carlos left the ladies to catch up and went to mingle with the guests.

"You and Carlito," Señora Medina questioned, watching Carlos walk away. "Is there something I should know?"

María smiled sheepishly. "He likes me. I like him. That's pretty much it."

"That's not it, María. I saw the way he was looking at you from across the room." Her tone changed as she lowered her voice. "Does he know about Rafael?"

"No, and he will never know." María looked around to make sure no one could hear the conversation.

"María, how can you say that? This man is clearly in love with you. How do you plan to keep your child a secret forever?"

"Señora Medina, I have a plan. I have thought about this already. Trust me."

"You're playing with fire, mi hija, and I don't like it. I'll be at your apartment first thing tomorrow morning so we can talk about this."

María reached out for Señora Medina's hands and squeezed them. "I would love to have you over for Christmas breakfast tomorrow. Everything will be fine. You'll see."

María spotted Carlos and excused herself to go join him. She enjoyed being by his side while they made the rounds greeting guests. Carlos was naturally charismatic and had many friends. María felt special that he made sure everyone knew they were a couple, including the shameless bachelorettes looking for a husband.

As the night progressed, they danced and ate and had a great time. All eyes were on María, not only because she was with Carlos, but her dress was also so exquisite. Even the hostess displayed a hint of envy.

"How you managed to make such a beautiful dress while working all of those long days this month is beyond me. Where did you find the time?"

"She's just that amazing," Carlos quickly responded. Eva stared at the couple as the two smiled and gazed into each other's eyes. It was obvious things were getting serious between the two, and Eva wasn't sure if she liked that. Her little brother always had a soft heart for strays, and she wasn't sure if this one was any different from the others. Yes, María was a hard worker and kind-hearted, but she came from little. She was nowhere near the same class as the Alvarez family.

"Wow! Look at Cinderella," Alejandro walked up to María, looking at her a little too intensely. "It is amazing how the right dress can make even a simple girl look decent." Carlos pulled María closer to him.

"Are you drunk already, Hermano?"

"What are you talking about?" Alejandro replied, still looking at María with a savage grin. "The party hasn't even started yet, but it will very soon."

"Let's go get something to drink," Carlos said as he led María to the beverage cart and away from his brother. "I'm sorry, cariña. My brother can be an idiot when he's had too many coquitos."

María giggled, "Nothing can bother me tonight, Carlos. Not even the great Alejandro." Caressing his face, her tone became serious. "I am with you, and that makes me very happy. No one else matters."

Fighting the urge to kiss María's in public, Carlos took her hand and brought it up to his lips. "*You* make me happy," Carlos whispered and looked at María with love in his eyes.

María was lost in the moment that she didn't notice a woman trying to get her attention from across the room until she was right in front of her.

"Ana?" María was shocked to see her childhood friend.

"I've been trying to get your attention. I can't believe it's you . . . here in Miami!" Ana spoke loud and fast, barely catching a breath. They kissed each other on the cheeks and loosely hugged. Their friendship fizzled after Ana moved to the United States and became a model. María hadn't seen her since before Rafael was born. As far as she knew, her friend knew nothing about that part of her life.

"What are you doing in Miami?" Ana asked as she looked at María, shocked to see her looking elegant.

"I moved here in the spring." Carlos cleared his throat to signal that he wanted an introduction. "Oh, I'm sorry. This is Carlos Alvarez."

"I know who you are," Ana responded with a flirtatious smile. "My husband was looking in to accounting services for when he opens his firm. He is a paralegal and almost finished with law school. He saw your company but decided on a bigger accounting firm that could handle the business." Carlos didn't know how to respond to that comment. He handled many large companies in the Miami area very successfully.

"Husband?" María's face lit up. "You're married, Ana?"

"Yes!" Ana held out her hand to display the single carat diamond cluster ring. "We got married two years ago, and we have a three-month-old baby boy."

María leaped in to Ana's arms and gave her a firm hug. She was truly happy for her friend. "I am a lucky girl, María." Ana looked around the room. "He's here some-where. You know him. He's from back home."

María was sure she didn't know Ana's husband. The last five years she spent back home were spent in seclu-sion. Between spending the pregnancy locked in a room and afterward only going to work and church, María interacted with no one.

Suddenly, Señora Medina rushed up to María and grabbed her arm. "María, you must come with me."

"What's wrong?"

"Please, trust me. We have to go."

Carlos looked concerned. "Estella, is there something wrong? You look like you've seen a ghost."

It was at that moment that María spotted what brought fear to Señora Medina. A chill went down María's spine as she felt all the blood drain from her face.

"It can't be," María whispered under her breath as she saw the ghost of her past. Slowly coming toward her was a wagon full of hurt, lies, abandonment and rejection.

"Mi amor! There you are," Ana said as she reached for her husband's hand.

María's lips quivered as she said, "Antonio."

"Yes, I knew you would remember him," Ana laughed as she linked arms with Antonio, oblivious to the sudden awkwardness. María couldn't believe he was standing in front of her, even more handsome than the day he walked out of her life.

Carlos stepped close to María and placed his hand on the small of her back, causing her to jump. "María, what's gotten into you?"

María felt like her heart would jump out of her chest. Tiny beads of perspiration formed on her upper lip. *This can't be happening. This can't be real.*

"Hello María," Antonio finally spoke, eyes fixated on María, trying to connect with hers. So many times, she rehearsed what she would say if she ever saw him again but never could she have imagined that it would be in a setting like this.

"I see you've met my special guests," Alejandro said as he walked up to the group swirling the ice in his glass of rum.

"Alejandro, what is going on here?" Carlos was starting to get angry. It was clear there was a lot of tension in the room, but no one was explaining anything. The music seemed extremely loud in María's ears that she couldn't hear anything else.

"Carlos, this is Antonio Morales and his beautiful wife Ana. They are from the motherland." Laughing at his own joke, Alejandro nearly spilled his drink. Carlos extended his hand and properly greeted the man. "As a matter of fact," Alejandro continued, "I believe they are from the same town as our little seamstress here. María grew up with Ana." Alejandro paused for a moment and gave María a hard look. María pleaded with her eyes, begging Alejandro to not continue with his plan that was obvious to her by now. Despite seeing the tears welling up in María's eyes, Alejandro proceeded. "And Antonio here, is the father of María's baby."

"What," Ana shrieked. "Antonio is that true? I mean, María, I heard that you got pregnant and that that they kicked you out of Altagracia school for nuns, but I never heard who the boy was that got you . . ."

"Stop it," Señora Media snapped at Ana to stop her from continuing the public exposure of María's past. A tear rolled down María's face, giving herself away.

"See, Hermano, our little seamstress here is not the innocent we all thought she was," Alejandro said, laughing hysterically. By now, there were several people who overheard the interaction, including Eva, and now there was an audience.

María was afraid to look at Carlos and see the disappointment in his face. Carlos looked at Antonio and could see in his face that this was all true. He looked at María, waiting for her to say something to him, anything, but she never looked his way. Carlos pushed Alejandro out of his path and walked away. When María looked up, she saw him going out the front door.

"Carlos," María yelled, about to run after him when Señora Medina grabbed her arm.

"Let him get some air. He will be back."

María pulled her arm away from Señora Medina. "Don't talk to me. You did this. You told them, and you did this!" Anger fill her heart as she accused her mentor of now ruining her life. María noticed that the music had stopped, and she was the center of attention. Hours ago, she was the princess of the party, and now she was the shamed. She looked at Señora Medina again and whispered, "I will never forgive you for this."

María ran out of the house, hoping to find Carlos outside, but his car was gone. Down the street, she could see Antonio and Ana getting into their car. Of course, he would be making his escape. He didn't even stay to ask how his son was doing. He didn't even stay to see how *María* was doing. It was déjà vu, the feeling María felt of being completely alone, much like the last time she saw Antonio when he walked out of her life.

Suddenly, María felt someone grab her hand. It was Rosa, her dear friend who she had been horrible to. "Let me take you home," she said and walked her to the car. The moment Rosa started to drive away, María burst into tears and didn't stop until she fell asleep that night.

Chapter 16

For two days, María stayed in bed feeling sorry for herself. Rosa called a few times, but María couldn't manage the energy to have a conversation with her friend. She only stayed on the phone long enough to convince Rosa that she was fine. But she wasn't fine. Thoughts constantly ran through her head of how disappointed Abuela would be to know that her secret made its way to America, the shame that tarnished the Garcia name.

You can't hide from your sin. Your sin is who you are. Voices in her head said the same thing over again, reminding her that this was her life. She might as well have been wearing a sign on her forehead that said "sinner" because she felt like everyone knew and everyone judged.

As soon as it was ten o'clock, María made her way downstairs to the boutique. By then, the store was open, and Eva would be there so she could collect her things. María was nervous about talking to her and prayed that she would give her some time to find another place to live before completely evicting her. Although it pained her that she wouldn't be working at Eva's Fashions any-more, she didn't blame Eva at all. The scene at the party not only embarrassed Eva but also disrespected her in front of her family and friends. María presented a false identity and lied to a woman who was more than gra-cious to her. No one could forgive that, and María was sure of that.

Walking by Valerio Accounting without looking in was hard for María, but she couldn't help it. Surprisingly, Carlos wasn't there. The lights were still off, and there was a sign on the door stating they were closed until the New Year. Carlos never mentioned that he would close his business for the holidays. Perhaps the embarrass-ment from the party caused Carlos to close the office for a couple weeks. It was evident to María the effect her actions had on the people around her. Even Carlos was affected by her mistakes. Tears started to fill María's eyes at the thought of what her actions were doing to the man she cared for. She quickly wiped her eyes and walked into Eva's Fashions.

"Buenos días, Eva." Eva was stone-faced as María walked toward her, avoiding eye contact. "I've come to pick up my things." Eva didn't say a word, but her face said everything. María began to ramble, "I'm grateful for everything you've done for me . . . all that you have taught me. I never meant to lie to you, and I'm sorry you had to find out this way. I pray you will forgive me one day, and I pray that God blesses you because you have been good to me and—"

"Enough," Eva shouted, startling María and forcing her to look Eva in the eye for the first time since the party. "What is wrong with you, María? Why are you talking so much? And why are you late?" Confused, María started to explain, but Eva talked over her. "Hurry up and prepare the Vasquez gown. She will be here in twenty minutes for the final fitting." María couldn't understand what was happening. After everything that transpired at the party and all that was revealed, did Eva still want her to work for her? The two women stood in silence for what seemed to be an eternity. Slowly, Eva's stoic face relaxed, and compassion showed in her eyes.

"María, it is I who owe you an apology. I didn't know Alejandro was going to do what he did. I knew months ago about your past, but it wasn't from Estella. She never told me anything about your personal life. Don't blame her for this, and don't shut her out. Alejandro found out on his own when he saw that you and Carlos were spending a lot of time together. At that time, you two were just friends, but he could see the way Carlos looked at you that it would develop into something bigger. He wanted to make sure you came from a good family; God forbid you make him look bad." Eva took a step closer to María and held her hand. "This was not about you, María. Alejandro is my brother, and I love him, but he is a very prideful man who enjoys the spot-light, and if anyone threatens that in any way, he finds a way to eliminate the problem."

María put her head down, fighting back the tears. She was the problem, and her big secret would hurt the family and Alejandro's political career. She understood that, but she didn't understand why Eva still wanted her to work for her.

"I need you here, María. You don't have to run away because I am not letting you go."

"But Alejandro—" María interrupted.

"I will handle Alejandro." She responded firmly.

"But what . . . what about Carlos?" María's voice cracked.

"Carlos is being an immature boy. He hasn't answered my calls, and he didn't come for Christmas dinner either. He will be fine. You need to think about yourself right now. Stay with me at least until the summer. If you still feel like you should leave, I will help you in any way I can. But don't let what happened at my house cause you to hide your head in shame."

María wiped her eyes and shook her head in agreement. "Thank you, Eva. Thank you so much." María was grateful that Eva had compassion, but María's heart was breaking for Carlos. Her feelings for him went deeper than she thought, and knowing that he had gone into isolation because of her made her heart ache. How would she ever face him again now that she was staying in Miami? When he gave her the opportunity to explain at the party, María stood frozen and made him look like a fool. She was just as much of a coward as Antonio was. When it counted most to speak up, fear kept them quiet.

"Before I forget," Eva said, reaching for a gift-wrapped box under the counter. "Here is your Christmas present. I didn't get a chance to give it to you at the party. I hope you like it." María was overwhelmed by the gesture. After all that happened, Eva still thought enough of her to give her a gift. When she opened the box, there was a silk black and white polka dot scarf inside. María had never owned silk; it was a beautiful luxury. However, the polka dots reminded her of that fateful night and her dress. The site of polka dots only brought anxiety and self-loathing.

"What's wrong? Don't you like it?"

"It's beautiful, Eva, thank you. It's just the polka dots have a bad memory for me," María confessed.

"Then turn it around! When something bad happens, change the story into something good. So, polka dots signify a bad thing in your past. Change it! From now on, polka dots bring good luck. Think of it that way, and you will do better in life." María chuckled at the thought. Good luck was definitely something she was in need of these days.

María stayed and worked at the boutique the rest of the day and week. It was very busy with women picking up New Year's Eve gowns. Regardless of the busyness, customers found the time to comment and snicker when they saw María. The news about her had spread, and she was now the topic of community gossip.

Each night María would go upstairs to her apartment and cry, and each night the tears were less and less. The more people would talk about her and her life back home, the harder her heart became. Eva defended María on a few occasions out of guilt for what her brother had done, but at the end of the day, María knew that deep down, Eva saw her the same way the gossipers did.

On New Year's Eve, the boutique closed early, and the elite of Miami prepared for an exquisite party at the Deauville Hotel. María felt a hint of jealousy. Eva's Christmas party gave her a taste of upscale festivities. Although short-lived, María loved the feeling of attending such a soiree and being among the wealthy, even though she was not one of them. There was silence in the atmosphere that night because everyone was somewhere saying goodbye to the old year and celebrating the year to come with their loved ones. Being alone was agonizing, and all the negative thoughts came in like a flood.

It's your fault you're alone. This is how your life will be. You will never be part of the elite. You will always be a low-class, stained woman.

By the time it was midnight, María was asleep. Carlos left a bottle of Ron del Barrilito rum in the cabinet at Thanksgiving that María indulged in for the first time. She never understood the fascination people had with alcohol until a few minutes after her first glass. The soothing subtle sweetness warmed her from the inside and quieted the voices in her head. New Year's Day was nothing different. María spent the day at home where normally she would go to church. Knowing how the news spread in the community about her personal shame, she didn't want to subject herself to the whispers.

Monday morning, María woke up early, refreshed, and determined. She made the decision to honor Eva's request and continue working for her through Communion, prom, and wedding season. In the meantime, she would save money and make plans to move back home. It would be easier to face the gossipers back home than it would be in Miami. Having to face the community, Alejandro, and Carlos would be hard for six months, but it was better than having to endure it for her lifetime.

As María finished her morning coffee, there was a knock on the door. It was probably Eva. Sometimes she would stop by the apartment to meet with María and discuss business before opening the boutique. When María opened the door, her heart leaped.

"Carlos?" A mixture of emptions quickly overwhelmed María. Although she was shocked to see him standing at her door, María was happy to see Carlos. She wanted to be angry with him for disappearing after the party and not giving her the opportunity to explain, but the fact that he was at her door warmed her heart.

"Can I come in?" Carlos wasn't sure how María would receive him. His pensive look spoke volumes. María realized that Carlos was there to officially end their relationship, and she motioned him to enter. After all the tears that had been shed the past nine days, somehow María still had more to spare. Tears welled up in her eyes, and she took a deep breath before turning around to face him.

Carlos paced back and forth in the small apartment, looking for the words to say. Eyes focused on the carpet to avoid making eye contact and seeing the tears in María's eyes. Suddenly, after taking another deep breath, María found the courage to start the conversation.

"I'm sorry, Carlos. I never meant to hide my past from you. You have been so good to me, and I will always remember that. You didn't deserve what happened at the party. The humiliation should have been all mine, not on you. Eva has asked me to stay until the summer, which I have agreed to do. After that I will return home to my country and my son."

Carlos quickly looked up once María announced she would be leaving, revealing his own watery eyes. Their eyes locked for what seemed like eternity, and although neither uttered a word, their hearts spoke to each other. It was at that moment, María realized that she had fallen in love with Carlos, and breaking up would be harder than she thought. Without saying a word, Carlos turned around and walked out the door. María understood his pain and anger. She deserved that response.

María covered her eyes, trying to fight back the tears, but they made their way through. Broken-hearted, she stood in her living room and wept silently. *He'll never forgive me.* After a minute, María uncovered her eyes to see that Carlos had come back and was standing there with someone beside him. María's legs weakened, and she fell to her knees. "Rafael!" Her little boy ran into her arms, and she held him tight. "Precioso, you're here . . . I can't believe you're here." Joyful tears overcame María. When she looked up, Carlos was smiling, and Señora Medina was with him in tears.

Standing up, María questioned, "I don't understand. What has happened?"

"María," Carlos began, "I was surprised when my brother revealed your past at the party. But I wasn't upset about your past. I was upset that you didn't trust me enough to tell me yourself. I had to get away and think, and I quickly realized that nothing has changed. My feelings for you are still the same." Carlos walked up to María and held her hand.

"I love you, María, everything about you. I called Estella the next day and told her my plan in confidence. I traveled back with her and met with some of my contacts. They helped me get papers for Rafael to bring him to you. A family should be together, and your abuela agreed.

"Abuela! You met my grandmother?" María said, catching her breath.

"Of course. Out of respect, I had to get her approval and her help to make this happen." Still holding María's hand, Carlos bent down on one knee. María's eyes opened wide, knowing what that position meant. Señora Media walked over and handed Carlos a small blue velvet box. Carlos opened the box to reveal a modest pear-shaped diamond solitaire ring. "María, will you marry me?"

'Yes, Carlos, yes!"

Carlos placed the engagement ring on María's finger and kissed her gently on her lips. "I'm going to make you happy," he whispered.

María was happy. Never did she imagine that things would turn out this way. Her heart was full, and she felt loved.

Acknowledgements

I am so thankful to God that I have finally finished this book! Different life hiccups throughout the years prevented me from finishing but here we are. Thank you to everyone that has been with me in this long journey, including:

My Florida family! Thank you for putting up with me all these years while writing this book. Specifically, my sister Stella; thank you for your constant feedback during this process. You understood my emotional rollercoaster with Maria.

To my beautiful young adult reviewer, Anaia Alicea. Thank you for your opinions, suggestions and encouragement while I was building the early chapters of the book. You helped me more than you know.

To my Pink sisters: Beauty Consultant Mercedes Bonilla, Sales Directors Lisa Collazo, Roslyn Codette-Rodgers, Maya Etayo and Pink Elite Senior Sales Director Sharon Miranda. You ladies have encouraged me so much through the years. Your determination, strength and success in your own lives were motivation for me and sparked a flame to bring this dream to fruition. I love you ladies!

Finally, "El Chapo"- My trusted friend and business partner. Thank for not giving up on me. Thank you for pushing me to the finish line. I couldn't have done this without you. I'm forever grateful.

♥Mimie